OREGON DESTINY

RACHEL WESSON

LONDONGATE PUBLISHING

CHARACTER LIST

The following are a list of the main characters in this book, the majority of whom you met in Oregon Bound - book 1.

Thompson family:
Pa - Paddy Thompson
Ma - Della Thompson
Eva - now Mrs. David Clarke
Rebecca and Johanna Thompson - the twins
Stephen Thompson

Other characters
Captain Scott Jones - Wagon Train Leader
David Clarke - now married to Eva Thompson
Rick Hughes and his nieces, Sarah and Carrie
Mrs. Long and her three daughters.
Freeman family - Pa, Ma, Sheila and her brother Joey

Bradley family - Pa and his daughter Gracie

Stan and his pregnant wife, Milly.

Mr Price and his son Almanzo

Mr. and Mrs. Newland

Paco, his wife Winona and their sons.

CHAPTER 1

$\mathcal{B}$ecky Thompson watched the leader of their wagon train, Captain Scott Jones, ride out of camp. He was alone for the first time in what seemed like ages. She hurried through the rest of her chores before telling her ma she was going to spend some time with her pregnant friend Milly. Milly was anxiously awaiting the birth of her first baby, and Ma encouraged all of them to spend time with the young mother-to-be, to help keep her spirits up.

Becky walked in the direction of Milly's wagon until she was out of sight. Then she turned and ran to where her pa's horses were hobbled.

"Come on, Ireland, we have to find Scott." The horse neighed softly, not loud enough to cause anyone to become alarmed. She rode slowly out of camp, not allowing the horse to canter until they were some distance away. She spotted Scott up ahead, his horse contentedly grazing while he stood staring into the distance. She rode up to him, causing him to turn quickly his gun cocked.

"Becky! What on earth? I could have shot you."

"But you didn't." She dismounted.

"What are you doing out here?" he asked. "Do your parents know where you are?"

"I told Ma I was going to see Milly. She won't check. I had to come. I had to see you."

"Why?"

"You seem to be upset. Is there something wrong? Something you are not telling us?"

"It's your imagination, Becky. My job means I must stay vigilant."

"This is more than that. Does it have something to do with that man, Mitchell, back at Fort Hall?" She knew she had hit a nerve from the look on his face. She wished he could be honest with her. "I am not a damsel in distress nor am I going to swoon. You are worried and I want to know why."

"Becky, leave it alone."

"But there is history between you and this Mitchell guy. I know you knew each other. Didn't you?"

"Yes."

"So that's why you got into the fight. It wasn't to protect mine and Eva's honor."

He looked at her before staring into the distance. She knew he didn't like to lie so she waited.

"That was part of it but you are right there were other reasons," he growled. "I am not willing to talk about them."

"I wish you would trust me. I am not a child."

He put out his hand and drew her to him. Pushing her hair gently back from her face, he looked in her eyes.

"I don't believe you are a child." He bent his head and kissed her on the lips. As before, the spark between them ignited. She wrapped her arms around his neck, clinging to him as heavenly sensations overtook her body. She wanted more yet she wasn't sure what that was. She moved closer to him, only their clothes separating them.

"Becky, I..." he groaned pushing her gently away. "Go back to your wagon. You aren't safe here."

"Yes, I am," she whispered as she nuzzled his neck, her lips making a track down to the top of his collar bone. Hearing him groan once more turned her limbs to liquid.

"Becky. Go. Now." He pushed her away, not too gently this time. She stumbled slightly as he moved away.

"But...you like me."

He stopped walking. His shoulders straightened as

he turned back toward her. "That's the problem. I like you too much. You and I aren't suited. There is no future in this, and I won't take your innocence."

She opened her mouth to protest but the expression in his eyes stopped her.

"Please go Becky. There is only so much temptation I can take."

She turned and ran, her cheeks flaming, tears running down her face. Not of hurt but of frustration. How could he think they didn't have a future together? What gave him the right to make that decision for her. Didn't her opinion count?

SHE MOUNTED Ireland as quickly as she could and rode back to their camp. Dismounting, she hobbled the horse before walking slowly back toward their wagon. She saw Johanna and Eva laughing with their ma over by the fire. Desperate to avoid them, she moved silently toward her tent. She didn't want anyone witnessing her tears. She rarely cried so they would be concerned. Her parents already had reservations about Captain Jones. She wasn't going to add any fuel to that fire.

She reached the tent without being seen. Lying down and pulling the covers over her fully dressed body, she pretended to be asleep when Johanna came in some time later. She waited until she heard her sister's soft snores before she opened her eyes. What did she have to do to convince Scott they were meant to be together? And what part did Mitchell play? Despite what Scott had said, he was worried, and she was convinced the horrible man from Fort Hall was the reason why.

CHAPTER 2

*H*e watched her run, his heart torn in two. He regretted his callous treatment of her but he only had so much self-control, and she felt so good in his arms. Her body melded to his, responding to his caresses instinctively, yet he knew her to be innocent. If only he was in a position to ask to court her. If he could offer her a stable home and a decent future he would, but that wasn't in his power to provide. He wondered if it ever had been, but any chance was long forgotten now that Mitchell had turned up. His face hardened at the thought of the man who had ruined his life once before. He wasn't about to let him get away again. But first he had a duty to take these travelers safely to Willamette Valley. Only once that was achieved would he deal with Mitchell.

He turned his focus to the journey ahead. They

should be able to replenish their supplies at Fort Boise even though it was a bit late in the year. They may even be able to replace the two horses he had shot. They had gone lame shortly after Rick was nearly killed crossing the river at Three Island Crossing.

It was a bit late in the year for the trappers to be hanging around the fort, but he had a feeling his old friend, Alberto, might be there. He would be able to tell him more about Mitchell, particularly how he escaped the hanging.

He mounted his horse and turned in the direction of the camp. He had to keep his distance from Becky. The chemistry between them was powerful and although he wanted to believe he had the will power to resist her, he wasn't so certain of his body. No woman had ever fascinated him for so long. Not even Kateri. Although he had loved her, their match had been arranged by the tribe. They had grown up together so it seemed natural to get married. He would have stayed happily married if he had been given the choice. But the passion he shared with Becky had never been there between him and his wife. There was nothing for it but to always insist someone accompany them. A chaperone.

CHAPTER 3

*B*ecky studiously avoided Scott. If he came near their fire to talk to Pa, she wandered off to see Milly or call on someone else.

"Why do you keep avoiding Captain Jones?" Johanna asked her, a curious look in her eyes.

"I don't."

"Yes, you do. You have gone from hanging on his every word to ignoring him. What type of game are you playing now?"

"I am not playing any games, Johanna. Leave me alone."

She wasn't going to cry in front of her twin. She had said enough about her love for Scott. She didn't want her sister's pity.

* * *

"THE NEXT STREAM we come to is about six feet deep. We will have to raise the wagons to cross it. We will set up camp now and then tackle it first thing in the morning. Agreed?" Captain Jones surveyed the group but Johanna noticed his gaze lingered on Becky. Her twin was studying the ground. Honestly, she wanted to bang both their heads together.

Instead, she caught the scared look on Milly's face. She couldn't do anything about Becky but she could help Milly. Johanna went over to reassure her. "We will be fine. We are so good at crossing rivers now we can do it in our sleep."

Milly looked unconvinced. She kept rubbing her bump and staring at the river.

"Come on, Milly, let's get some food. You will feel better after eating."

"Rick nearly died at the last river crossing."

Johanna didn't need reminding her fiancé had almost died, but she wasn't going to tell her friend that. She knew Milly wasn't thinking straight. She took her hand and led her in the direction of the food. "It's only a tiny little stream. Don't lose any sleep over it."

They raised the wagons ready for the morning. Johanna caught the look her parents exchanged. Surely, they weren't worried about the crossing. She watched as her pa gave her ma a quick kiss on the cheek before he went to check his cattle.

"What's wrong, Ma? Why are you frowning?"

"It's nothing, Johanna."

"Ma, tell me. I am not a child."

"Sorry, Johanna, of course you aren't. I am a little worried about our food supplies. I thought we would have more set by. I am sure I am fussing over nothing."

Johanna knew her ma wasn't the sort to get upset unless there was good reason. She must speak to Rick, maybe the men could go hunting.

THE NEXT MORNING, the crossing went well until the cattle started to move. Johanna watched her pa as he seemed to be pulling one animal. Captain Jones rode back over the river to check. Next thing a shot rang out, the sound reverberating around the valley. The animal slumped to the ground.

Johanna pushed Carrie's head into her skirt, her instincts to protect the young girl.

"It was the best thing to do, Carrie. It got stuck in quicksand. He would have died anyway but it would have been a slow death," Rick said. "Jones had no choice."

Johanna looked up at Rick who was still astride his horse. He knew how she felt about animals suffering. She smiled at him showing she understood Jones had done the right thing, but all the while inside she was cursing this journey. Just how many more people or animals would die before they reached Oregon.

"Come on children, let's see if we can find any choke berries. I read they grow in this area." Johanna looked up at Rick.

Rick flashed her a smile, which lit her up inside, before he blew her a kiss and headed back to help move the other cattle. He'd gone before she remembered she had meant to ask him about going hunting. It would be an excuse to seek him out alone. She missed his kisses.

THAT EVENING, they camped at the foot of a large hill. The grass was reasonable. Scott pushed his hair out of his eyes. The river crossing had gone well apart from the death of the animal. Tomorrow would be difficult not just because of the height of the climb but because the road was poor. He knew people were worried about the lack of provisions.

He stroked his stubble, watching Becky. She refused to acknowledge him and although he couldn't blame her, it stung. He wished more than anything he hadn't bumped into Mitchell. A couple of days earlier or later and Mitchell might not have been at Fort Hall. He could have gone to Becky's parents, told them his plans to set up a horse ranch, the number of horses he already had and… Cursing silently, he picked up his blade and headed to the river. Unlike most wagon captains he hated whiskers, preferring to keep his face stubble free. It wasn't always practical but when the chance came to shave, he took it.

BECKY WATCHED as he headed to the river. She knew he would be alone. It took all her self control not to follow him. She had seen him looking at her earlier when she was pretending to ignore him, the pained expression in his eyes making her heart twist. Why was he insisting they had no future when he felt the same way she did?

CHAPTER 4

$\mathcal{B}$ecky yawned as she got up and ready for the day ahead. Captain Jones had warned everyone it would be a difficult day. She was driving the wagon today. Her heart beat faster as Scott came closer as if to talk to her but she purposefully turned her head. Unless he was ready to ask for her hand, she was going to continue ignoring him.

They ascended the hill carefully as the roads were very steep and rocky. The oxen were struggling. Becky tried to coax them to go faster but no matter what she did they wouldn't move. She couldn't see in front of her as the dust was too thick. She put on the brake, thankful she was the last wagon. There was no one behind her to plow into the back of them.

"What's wrong, Becky?"

"I can't get the oxen to move, Ma. Stay where you are. It's hard to see."

The good thing about the dust was it seemed to keep the mosquitoes at bay. When the wind blew and the dust cleared, they came back in force so any break was welcome. She inched her way to the oxen, feeling her way with her hands. She couldn't tell what was wrong. Maybe one of them was lame or something. Where was Pa when she needed him? He'd gone hunting with Rick. Johanna was driving Rick's wagon. She had no option but to wait until someone missed them. She groped her way back to the wagon.

"What is it?" Ma asked.

"I don't know. I don't think they are just being ornery. Nothing will make them move and—believe me —I tried force and sweet words."

"Poor creatures are exhausted. They have pulled our wagon faithfully for more miles than I care to think about," Ma sighed. "We will just have to wait a while until the others come back."

"Ma, can I ask you something?"

"What?"

"Are you glad you came? I know you didn't want to leave Virgil.," Becky hesitated. "What do you think now?"

Her ma stayed quiet for a few minutes. Becky waited,

sensing her mother was trying to put her thoughts into words.

"If I am honest, I would say I wish we were still in Virgil. But, and this will probably sound a little funny given what we have gone through, it has been an adventure. I have learned a lot about myself, Paddy, and of course, you children during this trip. I think in many ways our family has grown closer. So, I guess, I can't say I am sorry we left."

Becky sat in silence pondering her ma's words.

"What about you, darling? Do you wish you were back home in Virgil?"

"No, Ma. I was a silly girl when we lived there. I have grown up a lot. I needed to."

"Don't be so hard on yourself, Becky."

"But it's true. Eva was always the sensible one and Johanna the caring one. I was the wild one, chasing boys and what not."

"Don't remind your pa about the chasing boys bit, Becky. He likes to think his girls are still innocent little angels."

Becky smiled. "Sorry, Ma, but I don't think I was ever an angel."

"I wouldn't be without you for all the money in the world, Rebecca Thompson. Never forget that."

Their close chat was interrupted by some shouting from outside. Ma moved first and it was then Becky spotted the gun in her hand. She signaled Becky to stay quiet. Becky reached inside her pocket to check her knife was still there. She carried it everywhere just in case. It made her feel safer.

"Della, Becky, where are you?"

The women sagged in relief at the sound of Pa's voice.

"Here, Paddy, the wagon is stuck."

"Keep talking Della, so I can follow your voices. Can't see a thing in this wretched dust."

Ma kept talking, saying all sorts of silly things, until Pa and Rick found them. Ma stayed in the wagon but Becky led the men to the oxen.

"They just stopped, Pa, I don't know what's wrong with them. I couldn't move them."

"Looks like Henrietta is a goner. Pity as she was the best of them," Pa said sadly.

"Henrietta the ox is dead. How did I miss that?"

"Don't blame yourself, Becky. She may have still been breathing when you last checked. Poor girl is worn out."

"What will you do? How will you replace her? We will have to unyoke the oxen but with this dust…" Rick's voice trailed off.

"We will have to wait until later when the dust has died down. Rick, can you ride and find the rest of the train and tell them where we are?" Pa asked.

"I can't leave you here alone."

"You have to. Becky and Della are armed. We will be fine. Go."

When Rick hesitated, Becky added, "Please go, Johanna and the others will be worried."

"I will be back soon. Don't move." He smiled at his own joke before feeling for his horse, mounting and riding slowly away.

IT TOOK a few hours for the dust to clear and help to arrive. Pa used the time to sleep, her ma sewed while Becky wrote to Granny. She wasn't as good a correspondent as Johanna, but she found by writing, she could lay out her heartache on the paper. It made her feel slightly better writing it out. She hadn't decided whether she would post it. Johanna had told her a while back what their granny said about the type of man she needed. Someone who would keep her in her place, not allow her to rule the roost. She knew her granny didn't mean a man who would mistreat her or put her down. She meant someone who was strong enough to stand up for himself and not let her have her own way all the time. Granny had been right. She shuddered thinking of the life she had wanted. Once all she thought about were boys and new dresses. She had purposefully sought out the richer boys with the idea of settling in a nice house. How shallow she'd been.

Looking down at her pants, she couldn't help smiling. If her granny could see her now. She wasn't even wearing a dress, never mind the latest in fashion. What would her granny think of Scott Jones? Somehow, she thought she would approve.

CHAPTER 5

*R*ick arrived back with her brother-in-law, David. Captain Jones followed them leading an ox.

"Mr. Bradley gave you his last one. If we lose any more, we will have to either dump a wagon or try getting the milk cows to pull it."

Becky laughed thinking he was joking but when no one joined her, she stopped. "You aren't serious."

"Deadly."

"But they aren't trained to pull a wagon," she protested.

"Well, its either that Becky or you carry everything."

She stopped arguing. It might never happen after all. At the moment, they couldn't talk without ending up in a fight, so it was better to stay out of the discussion.

"Come on, girl, let's go make some coffee. We both could do with some, and I am sure the men wouldn't say no."

Becky followed her ma some distance away from the workers.

"Becky, you need to stop baiting Captain Jones. He isn't interested."

Becky's head jerked up wanting to deny her ma's words, but she didn't. Instead, she stared over her ma's shoulder at the man she loved.

"I know it's not what you want to hear, but it's for the best. Now, let's concentrate on getting our chores done. No better cure for a broken heart."

Her ma might be trying to be nice, but really, what did she know? She had only ever loved her pa and given they had married younger than Becky was now, she was hardly an expert on affairs of the heart.

THE WEATHER HAD TURNED MUCH COLDER. Johanna was busy turning one of Becky's wool dresses into dresses for Sarah and Carrie. Becky wasn't wearing it and the girls were freezing in their calico ones. It was a difficult project and she wasn't holding out much hope for the finished product. It might not look very fashionable, but at least, it would keep them warmer.

"David said we have to use a windlass to get up that mountain tomorrow," Eva commented.

"What's a windlass?" Johanna asked as she looked up from her sewing.

"It's a bit like a fishing rod. They use one wagon to haul up the rest." At the blank looks on the faces surrounding her, Becky explained further. "The men and oxen take a wagon up to the top of the hill, they empty it and then stake the wagon with one set of wheels running freely. They tie a strong rope around the axle and then lower the rope down the hill. The men below tie the rope around the first wagon. Once they give the signal, the men at the top use the oxen to turn the wheels until the wagon they are carrying reaches the top. Then they do the next and the next until all the wagons are done."

"I don't like the sound of that. Couldn't we fall out?" Milly asked.

"Milly, they aren't going to let you travel in the wagon. We have to walk."

Becky knew Milly was apprehensive. Her friend had confided she was having nightmares about the baby coming in the middle of nowhere. She was finding the trail difficult, the extra weight of the baby making her tired.

"Milly, why don't you let me fetch your water and do some of the other heavier chores. Johanna is the best at sewing but I can make some baby clothes if you want. We can all chip in."

Milly squeezed her hand, her gratitude shining from her eyes. "I am so glad we met up on this wagon train. I hope we get to live near each other in Oregon. I couldn't bear to never see you again."

The group went quiet for a few minutes, everyone caught up in their own thoughts.

"I guess it will depend on where the men file their claims," Eva suggested.

"Why do the men get to choose? Why can't we have a say? We are going to live there too."

"Becky, it's just the way of the world. You have to accept some things."

"No, Eva, I don't. I am not married yet. I won't marry someone who won't let me make my own decisions."

"So if Captain Jones asked for your hand tomorrow and wanted you to live on his claim on the moon, are you saying you would refuse to marry him?"

Becky wanted to stick her tongue out at Eva but she couldn't. Not in this company.

"Leave Becky alone, Eva," Johanna said, ever the peacemaker. "Milly, do you know what you are going to call your baby?"

While the others discussed baby names, Becky thought about Eva's comment. For all her talk about wanting to be independent, she knew she would follow Scott to the moon and back if he asked her. Was that what happened when you fell in love?

CHAPTER 6

*J*ohanna took a break from sewing to go check on the children. Carrie was asleep and Sarah was reading. Stephen and Almanzo were playing some sort of card game.

"Is everything all right over here?"

"Yes, Jo," the children chorused.

"Good night then. Stephen and Almanzo, it's time for you to get back to your tent. Ma will be checking on you soon."

"I forgot to do something. Pa is going to kill me." Stephen ran before explaining to the others what he hadn't done. Johanna smiled. Her brother was never going to change, always easily distracted he was forever getting into trouble with Pa.

She kissed the girls goodnight before deciding this was a good time for her to have a talk with Almanzo

Price. He appeared to be fine but being abandoned by your parents at the age of ten had to have an effect. Particularly when they had left him to die. But looking at him playing with Stephen and the girls, you wouldn't know he had a sad history.

She didn't like to make it obvious she was checking up on him. Not in front of the other children.

"How are you feeling?"

"Fine, thanks, Jo."

Although his words were what she wanted to hear, she guessed from his tone, he was saying them just to please her. "You know you can talk to me, don't you? Or Rick."

"Yes."

"What is it? I can see you are troubled. Can't you tell me? I may be able to help." Johanna kept her eyes on him but he didn't look at her. His eyes were focused on the ground.

"Do you think my parents are waiting for me in Oregon?"

Johanna's stomach turned. "I have no idea, darling. I wish I had but I just don't know."

"You think they are dead, don't you?" Almanzo asked in a quiet voice.

"Well…yes, if I am honest, I think they are. You've seen how hard this trip is and that's when we are working together. I can't imagine traveling this road alone."

He kicked at a pebble, his shoulders slumped over. She risked putting an arm around him. Ten was a prickly age, particularly for boys. They wanted to be treated as men but sometimes they needed a hug.

"Almanzo, I know it is hard for you. I've seen you checking the graves."

He colored guiltily.

"I don't know what is ahead of us but you will always have a home here with us," Becky continued. "Rick has told you that too."

"Yeah Jo, but when your own babies come, you won't want us around."

She took him by the shoulders and turned him to face her. Putting a finger under his chin, she forced him to meet her eyes."I promise you we will always want you. If we are blessed with children, we will need some help. I couldn't imagine a better helper than you."

Her heart grieved for him as doubt and hope mingled in his eyes. If she caught hold of his parents right now, she could kill them herself. Who would ever make a child believe they were unwanted and unloved?

"I mean it. It's not just words. You know I don't lie to you," she said.

He gave her a hug, his tears soaking into her dress.

"I promise, Almanzo, I will never, ever let you go

unless you want to leave. Rick feels the same." She swallowed hard to get rid of the lump in her throat.

"Thank you." His reply was muffled by her skirt. She pulled him closer as her own tears fell into his hair. They stayed silent for a while, both recovering their composure.

"Now tell me, before you came on this trip did you go to school?"

His shoulders went rigid.

"Nope. Pa said I was needed at home."

"Well, you will have a lot to catch up on then."

He untangled himself from her skirts quickly just as she intended.

"I ain't going to school like a child. I am going to help Rick work on the farm."

Johanna laughed. "Rick won't be much of a teacher if his own children aren't in the school. You have to keep the side up you know."

"Aw, do I really? Can't I just learn at home. School's boring."

"Learning is never boring, Almanzo."

"Yes, ma'am." His facial expression showed he clearly disagreed with her.

CHAPTER 7

avid and Scott were up ahead of the wagon train, trying to find some provisions. They hadn't been lucky with their hunting and the children's bid to find berries wasn't too successful either. David sensed it wasn't a lack of food accounting for Scott's bad mood. "What's on your mind?"

"What do you mean?"

"Scott, we've become friends on the trail. I know there is something bugging you and I want to know what. Especially if it is to do with the safety of the train," David wasn't at all sure Scott would tell him. Eva had insisted he try to talk to him. Becky was worried about him and had—unusually for her—confided her worries to Eva. "Is it anything to do with the man back at Fort Hall?"

"Why is everyone asking about him? He was just a no-good stranger with a dirty mouth."

David raised his eyebrows at Scott's tone. "Well, part of that is true. He did have a dirty mouth but he wasn't a stranger, was he? Becky said you knew him."

"Becky doesn't know what she's talking about."

"Funny, Eva said you called him by name. Is this a new skill you have? The ability to know a man's name even though you have never met before." David used a teasing tone trying to break through the shield Jones used to protect himself. He guessed the man had been through a bad time in his past. He was fair and a great leader but he rarely discussed anything personal.

"Okay, so I knew him, it was no big deal."

"I think it was Scott. We have been through some difficult situations. Harold and his friends and then that awful man Price. I have never seen you use your fists on anyone, yet you came back from Fort Hall looking like you took on a brown bear and came off worse. So tell me."

Captain Jones stayed silent.

"Go on Scott. It may help to talk. I owe you."

"No, you don't."

"Yes, I do. You stood by me when few others did. From the start, you didn't use my past against me so why should I use yours against..." David could have kicked himself. He had gone too far. Eva had told him the story Mitchell had said but he shouldn't have mentioned it. So much for letting Jones open up. His face had totally closed down. "Jones, tell me. I might be able to help."

Captain Jones examined David's face before he nodded, pointing to some trees up ahead. "Let's water the horses up there."

David followed to the trees and biting his tongue waited for Jones to speak.

"You're right. I knew Mitchell but we were never friends. It was a shock seeing him at the fort. I thought he was dead."

"I take it you weren't pleased he wasn't."

"That's an understatement, David. I have no wish to harm my fellow men, but for Mitchell, I would make an exception. That man has the black heart of a devil."

"Why did you think he was dead?" David asked.

"He was supposed to hang for his part in a massacre."

"Of Indians?"

Jones whirled around, the expression of rage on his face making David take a step back.

"Would it matter?"

"Scott, this is me, remember. I don't care if you got pink, white, blue or black skin. What on earth?"

Jones paced a bit then he apologized. "Sorry David.

My brain doesn't work straight when it comes to Mitchell."

"Don't know about you but my legs could do with a rest. I am going to sit by this bank for a while. You take your time and tell me when you want."

CHAPTER 8

*D*avid sat and waited a few minutes, his mind whirling. A massacre? A white man wouldn't be sentenced to death for murdering Indians at least not by any court he ever heard of. It was wrong but that was the way of the world. So this man must have killed white people? But why would they let a mass murderer walk free? This wasn't the civilized USA but still, surely, they had similar rules out here. Just what type of place was Oregon going to be. If they didn't abide by the same rules as the states he had come from, would Eva be safe? Would any of them?

Jones sat near him, breathing heavily. "I haven't spoken about this in some time. I would prefer if the rest of the group didn't know the details."

David nodded his agreement.

"I grew up not far from here. My family traveled in

one of the first wagon trains to Oregon. If you think the trail is bad now, it was a thousand times worse back then. There were no trails or signs to follow. My pa and the men with him just followed their instinct." Jones swallowed hard. "One night, our wagon train was attacked and everyone in it was killed. I only escaped as myself and my older brother, Tom, had gone fishing. We wanted to surprise our ma with fish for breakfast." Jones' voice quivered but David didn't move.

"When we got back to camp, everyone was dead. We buried them thinking we were safe. The Indians had taken what they wanted and wouldn't be back. We were wrong, David. Tom died trying to protect me."

Jones stayed silent for a little while. David waited until he couldn't wait any longer. "What age were you? Why were you spared?"

"I was five or six. I don't really know. Someone said I reminded this brave of his own child who had died the previous year. A lot of children had died and the Indians blamed it on the whites. In truth, they were right but not for the reasons they believed. The whites hadn't set out purposely to kill anyone but the Indians had never been exposed to white people's illnesses before. They couldn't fight back and many died. The Indians took their revenge."

"So he took you to live with them?" David asked.

"He did but I didn't stay. I couldn't. They had killed

my family. I ran away the first chance I got. The Shoshone took me in. I used to think all Indians were the same but they aren't. The different tribes go to war with each other all the time. The Shoshone were kind and treated me well. They taught me many of the skills I use to help people across the plains. I loved living with them."

"So this guy, Mitchell, was right,"David stated. "You married an Indian."

"Yes, Kateri was her name. We were happy and we had two children, a boy and a girl with a smile just like her ma."

David saw the water in Jones' eyes but took no notice. Instead, he moved toward the river. "My canteen is dry, just getting a refill."

When he returned, Jones flashed him a grateful smile. He had recovered his composure and continued with his story.

"The tribe was hungry. With the increase in emigrants, there was less food to go around. Shoshone survive by living off plants and animals and by fishing. What was once plentiful became scarce. I was curious about the white man's world. Some Canadian trappers used to visit the camp and one, Alberto, asked me to travel back with him. He was going to Mississippi to see the world as he put it. I left with Kateri's blessing. We knew she would not be welcome in the white man's world. I could bring back money to use at the forts. I had other reasons for wanting to go back East." Jones looked across the river into the distance. "That was the last time I saw my family."

"They died?"

"They were murdered." Jones' pain ravaged his face.

"Mitchell?"

"He was the cause. He is more responsible than the soldier who pulled the trigger."

CHAPTER 9

*D*avid's confusion must have been obvious as Jones explained. "Mitchell is what is known as a land pirate. He wants wealth but is not prepared to work for it. Instead, he steals it from those who are weaker than himself. From what I learned, at first, he sold emigrants false claims. But there was too much work in that. Instead, it was easier to dress up like an Indian and lead an attack on a wagon train. He tried not to leave survivors but in the last two attacks, he failed. For a while his strategy worked. The soldiers were ordered to put down the so called Indian rebellion. They attacked our camp when the men were out hunting. It didn't matter there were only old men, women and children left behind. They killed everyone."

"I don't know what to say."

"Nothing you can say. When I led my first wagon

train back, my brother-in-law was waiting for me. He told me the full story. Mitchell had recruited a number of Indian braves who he plied with cheap booze. He worked on their hatred of white people so there were Indians in the attacks. The ordinary Shoshone people were not responsible but that didn't matter to anyone. What did Price say? The only good Indian is a dead one."

"Price doesn't speak for all of us. How was Mitchell found out?"

"I brought him in. I wish I had killed him when I had the chance. I convinced my Shoshone brothers the white man would take his revenge on Mitchell. The captain at the fort promised me he would hang."

"Yet he didn't."

"He won't get away the next time," Jones vowed.

"You can't go after him. They will hang you for murder."

"They will have to catch me first. That man has almost fifty lives on his conscious, not including those white people he killed"—he spat on the ground—"he has to pay."

"I know you tried the right way before, but why not try again? Captain Weston was helpful last time. He might know how to get Mitchell put away or hanged."

"The army isn't interested in Mitchell and other men like him. You've seen their reaction to Indians. It is only a matter of time before the Indians who have lived here for centuries will be a part of history. The newspapers back East are full of stories of Indian attacks."

"But they have been helpful to us."

'That's not going to make the front page of any paper. Bad news sells, my friend."

"But what of Becky? You cannot make her a widow before she is even twenty."

Captain Jones's eyes clouded over with pain. "Becky will never be my wife. I don't have anything to offer her."

"But what of your plans for a horse ranch? I thought you wanted to settle in Oregon. I thought you had some horses already."

"I do and I did but that was before Mitchell. He changes everything."

"So are you giving up on the wagon train families as well as Becky?"

"Of course not. I made a promise to get you all to Oregon. I always keep my word," Jones responded angrily.

David stood up. It was time to get back before Eva got worried. What he heard had shocked as well as angered him. He hated injustice more than anything else in the world. But he wasn't about to let his new friend make a huge mistake. If he killed Mitchell now, it would be cold blooded murder.

"I expected more from you, Jones. This Mitchell man

already destroyed your life once. Now you mean to let him do it again?"

David didn't wait for an answer but mounted his horse, turned it back toward the wagon train and rode off leaving Jones sitting at the river. Alone.

CHAPTER 10

*H*e stared at the river for ages after David left. He couldn't really blame his friend for getting angry. It wasn't his family who had been murdered. He closed his eyes seeing his wife as she had been that last day. She'd stood smiling, holding the baby in one arm and little Crawling Bear's hand in the other. Crawling Bear was crying. He hadn't wanted him to go but he had promised the boy he would bring him back something special.

* * *

HE OPENED his eyes sensing he was being watched. His Indian brother, Paco, stood nearby waiting. He embraced him, both men holding on to each other for a long time.

"I saw you with white man. I waited for him to leave."

"He is a friend, a good man, named David. Thank you for coming, Paco."

"I got your signal. Why do you need to see me?"

Jones smiled. His wife's brother had always been a man of few words. To outsiders it may seem like he wasn't happy to see him but they were close friends. Closer than most brothers.

"I saw Mitchell—Black Heart Devil."

Paco's eyes blazed with hatred. "I heard whispers he was at Fort Hall but none of my men have seen him."

"I saw him." He flexed his hand, the scars on his knuckles evidence of the fight he had with Mitchell.

"Yet he still lives?" Paco scowled.

"I know you want him dead. I do too. Not just for Kateri and my children but for her sister too. I know it hurts you to be the only one left." Scott coughed as his voice was shaking. "I couldn't kill him in front of all those witnesses. I have a job to do first. I must take these people to Oregon. Then I will deal with Mitchell."

"Maybe we should deal with Mitchell for you. You have other priorities."

Paco's tone was like a spark to his anger.

"It's not like that," he spat back.

His friend's eyes narrowed making him rein in his anger. He tried to speak rather than snarl. "I made a promise and I always keep my word. Once the families are safe, I will handle it."

Paco shrugged his shoulders.

"You cannot go after Mitchell, you know our people will pay too high a price," he continued.

"Our people? Do you still feel that way?" Paco asked, his tone suggesting he was mildly curious but the expression in his eyes speaking the truth.

"Of course I do. We are brothers."

"It is good to know you still feel this way." Paco stared at him for a few minutes. "I heard your friend ask you about a woman. A white one."

Jones turned away from Paco. He didn't want his brother-in-law to see the emotions on his face. It was too late.

"You love this woman. Do not lie. I can read your face as always brother," Paco put his hand on Scott's back. "Kateri would not want you to live alone forever."

"Yes…I love her. But it is not that simple."

"Why? She does not want to share your blanket."

He laughed out loud at the thought of asking Becky to share his blanket. She would probably jump at the chance to live with the Indians for a while. She was always eager to shock people and try new things.

"No, she would if I asked. But she is young."

"How old?"

"Seventeen summers."

"That is not young. She is woman and ready for a man."

"Not in white man's world," he corrected. "Anyway, it doesn't matter what age she is."

"Because of Mitchell?"

"Yes. Kateri will not rest until he pays for what he did."

"Kateri or He Who Runs?"

He squirmed, not only because Paco had used his Shoshone name but because his question had hit the mark as usual. Who was he seeking vengeance for? Himself or his family? His wife had been a peace-loving woman. She hadn't wanted any part in the killing of whites even those who treated their people with little respect.

"Kateri believed for every white man who dies, a hundred Shoshone would die in his place," Paco reminded him.

"That is why you cannot kill Mitchell. I am a white man."

"But your world doesn't see you as white, do they?"

CHAPTER 11

*A*lthough he knew his brother-in-law often saw things others didn't, his perception surprised him. He stayed silent waiting for Paco to explain.

"I heard whispers but also spoke to Alberto. He told me of the issues with your family. They refused to believe you were Scott Jones, son of Matthew Jones."

He couldn't argue. What Paco was saying was true. His father's brother had refused to accept him. His uncle Jerry insisted his entire family had been murdered in the massacre. Jerry said he would have him arrested if Scott kept insisting he was his nephew. His uncle was wealthy and had a lot of power in the small town. Jerry seemed to think he was only interested in his father's money but Scott wasn't. He'd been looking for a family. Jerry had thrown him out on the street. His aunt had been slightly kinder but when she heard Scott had grown up with Indians and had a family, she too had turned her back.

"You are right. They didn't believe me. They don't matter."

"But their rejection has increased your hatred of Mitchell. You blame him for taking both your Indian family and the rejection from your white family. Your friend says you should not let him ruin your life again. I think he is right."

"He is wrong as are you," he growled. "I will not stand by and let Mitchell live."

"So now you are the all-powerful one? You are in charge of this man's destiny?"

Frustrated, he refused to answer Paco and instead, turned to go back to his horse.

"He Who Runs, cannot run away from his own head."

"What would you have me do?" Scott twirled around, his voice full of emotions. "Don't you know how much I want to marry Becky and have some children who grow up in safety on our horse ranch. But Mitchell being alive changed everything."

"It is not Mitchell, it is you." Paco stared Scott down. "Keep your promise. Help the white people finish their journey and then set up your horse place. Your horses are in fine condition. My son, Walking Tall, looks after them very well."

"Please thank him for me. If I can get away, I will come visit with you over the next few days. I would like to see Winona again too."

At the mention of Paco's wife's name, his friend's face grew pained.

"What is it?"

Scott sensed Paco's grief although the Indian's face remained impassive.

"Winona is sick. Our medicine man does not know what is wrong," Paco said in a voice choked with emotion.

"I may be able to help. There is a white woman in the wagon who is good with medicine. Will I ask her?"

Paco looked at him in silence, his expression doubtful. Scott couldn't blame him. The Indians had little experience of white people being helpful. But typical of Paco, his worry was for Scott rather than himself.

"How will you explain? You have not told these people your story."

"No, but I will, if it will help Winona. She was very good to me."

"She is fine woman and I do not wish to lose her. But I do not wish to create trouble either. There are many in our camp who do not like the white people. Chief tries to keep them in line but they are young and he is old."

"You sound ancient but you are only thirty summers."

"In my people, I am an old man." Paco's resigned tone worried him. Kateri's brother had always shared her hope and optimism for a peaceful future.

"Will I ask her?"

Paco thought deeply. Finally, he nodded. "Come tomorrow night. It will give me time to prepare our people, and also, to tell Chief about Mitchell. He will not be happy."

Scott stayed silent. What could he say? The Chief was right to be angry.

"I will meet you at the place of the two rocks. I will also ask my brothers to keep watch on your train." At the question in Scott's eyes, Paco explained the reason for vigilance. "In case Mitchell decides to follow you. Your people will not see them."

"Thank you, my brother." He embraced Paco. "Please ask your brothers to look for second white man. His name is Bill. He is this tall and has long whiskers. He has a mean heart too."

"Why can't you collect white man with good hearts?" Paco was teasing but they both knew he was trying to reduce the tension. Having Mitchell to contend with was bad enough without adding another enemy to the mix.

"I will see you tomorrow. Until then, keep well."

He watched as Paco left as silently as he came. Now he had no choice but to tell Becky his history. He doubted Hughes or Mr. Thompson would allow Johanna to come to the Indian camp alone with him.

CHAPTER 12

"Becky, Ma says not to be late for dinner this evening."

"I won't, Johanna, but what's so important?"

"Captain Jones wants to speak to us. I have to go, I promised to spend some time with Carrie and Sarah."

Johanna walked away quickly leaving Becky standing staring after her. Why did Scott want to talk to her family? She finished her chores and went to find her ma, but she didn't know what Scott wanted either. There was no sign of David. Pa thought it might have something to do with the trail as he had asked Rick to be there too. But if that was the case, why were the other travelers not included?

He couldn't be asking her pa for permission to court her. Could he? No, because he would do that in private.

But what did he want? She tried to stay busy but nothing could distract her mind. It was driving her to distraction.

* * *

EVA WAITED UNTIL LATE AFTERNOON, when Captain Jones told them to put up camp, to tackle David. He'd been in a funny humor since he'd come back from scouting with Captain Jones. Some of the men decided to go fishing but she asked David to stay behind with her. She indicated he should come into the wagon so they could talk in private.

"What is the matter with you? If we were back in Virgil, I would think you had lost a dollar and found a penny," she asked rubbing his back.

"Sorry, Eva. I have a lot on my mind."

"Share it with me. We are married. That's what couples do." Eva moved closer to him her arm caressing his neck. She knew he liked it. He said it calmed him down. "Is it the trip ahead? Are you worried the oxen might not make it?"

"Some of them certainly won't but it's not that. I can't tell you, Eva."

Her stomach tightened. What was so bad, he wouldn't share it with her?

"It is not my secret. I would tell you if I could but you

have to trust me. In time, you may come to find out. Until then, I promised not to say anything."

"Has this something to do with Captain Jones?"

"Yes."

"Him and Becky?"

"Eva, I said I couldn't tell you." David took her in his arms, kissing her on the neck. "I will share when I can, but for now, I can think of better things to do."

Eva let him draw her closer, his arms tightening around her, holding her pressed hard against him.

"Like what?" Eva whispered before she dissolved into giggles as his stubble tickled her.

"Maybe this…"

"Mm-hmm."

SOMETIME LATER, Eva tried again.

"Becky is worried about Captain Jones. She said he was acting differently toward her."

"I think we will all find out soon enough. I am not going to break his confidence, darling. No matter how much I love you."

Eva knew she had to be content with that. Having known David for years, she knew better than to test his loyalty. Once he gave his word, it was for keeps. She just hoped he was doing the right thing staying silent.

Someone knocked against the wagon. "Ma asked me to come get you. Captain Jones wants to speak to Pa and the family."

"Not the whole camp?" Eva asked through the canvas as she fixed her clothes.

"No, just us. I have to get Sarah and Carrie settled. I will see you in a few minutes."

Johanna had gone before she got a chance to ask her if she knew why they were meeting. She looked to David but judging by his expression he was as confused as she. They hurried to make themselves decent before heading toward the family campfire. Eva's cheeks flushed at the teasing look her ma gave her. Nobody else seemed to notice, thankfully, as all eyes were on Captain Jones.

CHAPTER 13

*J*ohanna was standing studying her but Becky pretended not to notice. She rebraided her hair, staying silent. Johanna sighed. "I thought you would change into something a little more becoming, Becky?"

"And show him how I feel, Johanna? Not likely. He either accepts me the way I am or not at all."

"Becky, darling, don't be so spiky. I was only making a suggestion. It's obvious how you feel about him, you have been on tender hooks all day."

"What could he possibly want to talk to Pa about?" Becky couldn't help asking. Did her twin think he was going to propose too or had she gone completely mad?

"You will soon find out. He is here."

Becky took a deep breath before following her sister out of the tent. She took a seat avoiding looking at Scott in case he saw the desperation in her eyes. She wanted him so badly.

* * *

"Thank you all for taking time to sit with me. I have a favor to ask and it's a big one," Captain Jones spoke to a point above their heads not looking at anyone directly. Becky had to sit on her hands, she wanted to jump up and hold his. To offer him support.

"You know we would do anything in our power to help you, Captain Jones. Have some coffee and a slice of cobbler."

"Thank you, Mrs. Thompson, for the coffee and the support. I have to be honest, my request is totally personal and nothing to do with the trail or our travels."

Becky's heart started beating faster despite the fact he had yet to look in her direction.

"Spit it out, young man. What do you want?"

"Mr. Thompson, I was wondering if I could borrow your daughter for a little while, this evening."

Becky nearly forgot to breathe. Stunned silence greeted his words.

"What I mean is, I have a friend who is ill and I would really appreciate Johanna's help."

Johanna, he had arranged this talk to speak about her twin. Of all the things she had expected, having nothing to do with her wasn't one of them. Nobody answered but simply stared at him. He continued as if he hadn't noticed their discomfort, "Johanna's proved herself to be an excellent nurse."

"Of course Johanna will help but where is this patient?" Becky's Pa asked the question on everyone's mind. "Why haven't you just brought them over? Why the secrecy."

Jones opened his mouth but nothing came out. He looked briefly to David.

"Captain Jones' friend is not part of our wagon train."

"Don't they have their own doctor on the train your friend is traveling on?" Pa continued.

Becky almost felt sorry for her pa as he looked confused. But she caught a look that passed between David and Scott. "This friend isn't white, is he?" she blurted out.

"No, Miss Thompson, she isn't."

"You want my daughter to treat an Indian?" The shock in her pa's voice might have been funny under other circumstances.

"Yes, Mr. Thompson I do," Scott swallowed audibly. "Perhaps I best explain."

"I think you should, lad," Ma answered patting Pa on his arm in a bid to stop him from storming off, Becky suspected.

"I am an orphan. Years ago, I came to live with the Shoshone Indians. The reason why is not important. What matters is they took me in, were very good to me. They gave me a name—they call me He Who Runs."

"They think you are a coward?" Ma's tone was full of disbelief. "Why?"

"No, Mrs. Thompson. I ran away from a horrible situation, hence the name. Now one of their people, a woman who was particularly kind, is ill," Scott ran a hand over his hair as he always did when he was was agitated or nervous. "Their own medicine man cannot save her. I don't know if Johanna might be able to but I would like to try."

"I will go with you," Johanna said firmly.

"No you won't, my girl. You are not going anywhere near an Indian camp. We all know what happens to young white women in those places."

"Pa."

"Paddy."

"Mr. Thompson."

All three spoke at once. Becky looked from Johanna to Pa to David. Why did David still call her pa Mr. Thompson? The abstract thought annoyed her so she pushed it from her mind.

"I can assure you Miss Thompson will be perfectly safe in my care. My brothers will not touch her," Scott spoke calmly but his eyes blazed at her Pa's reaction. "I would prefer not to bring any more men with me as there are some who could interpret that action as a show of force. But I will if you insist."

"Johanna isn't going anywhere without me," Rick insisted, taking Johanna's arm.

To Becky's surprise, her sister didn't shake it off but smiled up at her fiancé.

"I will go with Johanna," Becky surprised herself as much as the others by speaking out.

"You are better off staying here," Scott said.

His dismissive tone made her temper rise. "Why? You said yourself you didn't want to bring more men. I can handle a gun and a knife as well as any man."

"That has nothing to do with it. The less people who go the better."

"I am not people. I am her twin and I insist on going."

"Neither of my girls are going. I am sorry, Captain Jones, but I have to say no. It is far too dangerous," Pa said, although his expression wasn't apologetic.

Scott stood up. "Thank you for your time and your hospitality. I understand your reasons, although you are wrong."

CHAPTER 14

"Wait a minute. I will not sit by if there is a chance I can help this woman. I am going to help, Pa." Johanna had stood up to talk. "You brought me up to help our neighbors."

"But these people are not our neighbors."

"Why? Because they are not white?" Becky shut her mouth quickly fearing she had gone too far. Her pa didn't say anything but his face took on a rosy tint. Maybe she had hit close to the truth. She stood up and walked over to Johanna. "Both myself and Johanna will go. Rick, you may decide what you want to do. Pa, I am sorry but you are wrong."

"I agree with the girls. I think they should go. I trust Captain Jones and when he says they will be safe, he means it," David added. "The Indians have been very generous in their trades. I am certain the recent supply of fresh fish has helped us to stay healthy."

"Thank you, David," Captain Jones replied.

"Pa, please say yes? I do not want to go without your approval but I will."

Becky watched her pa's reaction to Johanna's plea. She saw her ma give him a slight nudge. Although her ma had stayed silent, it seemed she didn't agree with her husband.

"Okay you win. But, Jones, you better bring both my girls back in one piece. Otherwise, you will answer to me."

"Yes, sir."

"I am going with Jo." Rick stood and put his arm around Johanna's shoulders.

"Rick, I appreciate your sentiment. But it would be safer for everyone if you didn't. My brother does not know you." Before Rick could answer, Scott turned to David. "He has seen you, at the water speaking to me. He would not be surprised to see you with the twins as you are their brother-in-law."

David nodded.

Becky bit her lip. What would Johanna do? Rick looked mutinous. He would insist on going.

"I think it is best to follow Captain Jones' advice. He knows these people. Rick, I feel the same as you. I hate the thought of my girls going into that place without me. But…if it is safer, we should agree to it." Ma's sensible voice was designed to sooth ruffled feathers.

Johanna gave Rick a quick kiss on the cheek. "I think you should do what Captain Jones says too. Although I love you for your support and I will miss you dreadfully."

"I will stay behind. I don't like it but I won't put Johanna or Becky at risk." Rick's face showed his displeasure.

"We need to go now. The time is wasting," Captain Jones said.

"I must pack some things. Becky, can you help me, please?" Johanna said, reaching up to kiss Rick on the cheek.

CHAPTER 15

*D*avid and Captain Jones escorted the women back to their wagon to collect what they needed.

"Did your friend mention what could be wrong with the woman?" Johanna asked. "It would be helpful to know what to pack."

"No, sorry."

"I will just pack a bit of everything then. I hope we can help her. Have you explained that I am not a real doctor?"

"Yes, Miss Thompson, but Indians don't set much store by fancy titles," Captain Jones replied. "I have also told my brother you will do your best but the woman could still die. Do not be afraid. He knows the risks."

"Who is this woman?" Becky bit her lip at her tone. She hadn't meant to sound so belligerent. Scott looked at her, his raised eyebrows the only acknowledgement of her tone.

"Her name is Winona. Her husband is my closest friend, the brother of my wife."

Becky paled as the ground swayed under her feet. His wife?

Scott took her elbow and held it until the world stopping spinning. "I will explain later. For now, please put your questions aside and help your sister," he whispered tersely.

"Where is the camp?" David asked.

"It is some way away. We will ride at first and then leave our horses near some trees and walk the rest of the way. Paco will have some men watching us, one will stay with the horses.

"Why can't we just ride into the camp?" David asked.

"The Indians fear the white man. To ride into the camp at night would create panic."

Becky had a feeling that wasn't all the story but she wasn't about to challenge him now. He had said he would explain later. She had to have patience.

Becky rode behind Scott with David sharing his horse with Johanna. She used the opportunity to nuzzle close to him, his strong body helping to keep her fears at bay. She knew he wouldn't take them anywhere danger-ous. Yet her mind kept going over the stories Harold

Chapman had told them, back when they lived in Virgil, about Indians taking white girls for slaves.

THE MOON LIT up the clear night. Thankful it was dry, Becky tried to see if there was anyone watching them but she couldn't see anything. They reached the grove of trees Scott had mentioned. Jumping down, she waited for David to help Johanna. She had suggested her twin wear pants but she'd declined.

David carried Johanna's bag and they turned to walk when Johanna gave a small scream. Becky looked up instantly to see three Indians staring at them. They were riding horses yet nobody had heard them come near. At least they hadn't. Scott didn't look surprised.

"This is Johanna, the lady I told you about. Her sister, Becky, and their brother-in-law and my friend, David."

The Indian looked them in the face before he said something to Becky.

Scott answered back but as they spoke a different language Becky didn't know what he had said.

"It's rude to speak when we don't understand you," Becky said glaring at Scott. "What did he say?" she asked.

"Becky, it is better you do not know."

"I want to know." Becky didn't stamp her foot but her tone spoke volumes.

"He asked why pretty lady made herself look like ugly boy."

David and Johanna laughed but Becky didn't find his comments amusing. She glared at the Indian. He said something else to Scott before walking away laughing.

"What did he say?"

"I am not telling you. Come on let's move out."

The group followed their Indian guide. The other two Indians remained behind staring at them but not saying anything.

CHAPTER 16

*B*ecky watched Paco as he led the way. His sister was married to Scott. What did she look like? Were they happy? Did they have children? Would she meet his family at the camp? She wished now she had stayed with her ma and pa. She didn't know if she could meet Scott's loved ones and pretend to see him as just their wagon train captain. Surely his wife would see by her face and actions she was in love with him. She started to fidget as she always did when nervous.

"Becky, what's wrong?"

"Nothing."

"It's something. Tell me, now before we get to the camp. You are not in danger. Do you believe that?" he asked softly so only she could hear.

"Yes," she lied. While she didn't think anyone would

kill her, she also didn't believe his wife would welcome her arrival.

"Tell me what you are thinking."

"Scott, will your wife be there?" Not waiting for his answer, she blurted. "How could you kiss me like that when you are married?"

"Was married. My wife died some time ago."

The rigidness of his body told her he was telling the truth but that there was more to the story. He had his reasons for not telling her more so she had to respect them. Although she was sorry the woman was dead, a part of her was glad he was free. Immediately the thought hit her, she felt awful. How could she think that way?

THEY WALKED QUITE a bit before they came upon the camp. It was very quiet. A couple of men were standing outside one of the lodges. Scott directed his group over to them.

"This is the Chief, his medicine man and some other important braves. Show respect," Scott whispered before moving forward to greet them himself. He clasped the old chief's hand before he was engulfed in a warm embrace.

"It has been too long, my friend."

"It is good to see you too, Chief. These are my friends, here to help Winona." Scott caught the frown on the medicine man's face. "My friends were taught some white man medicine. It may work for Winona too. You are very kind to let us try."

Scott smirked to himself. The medicine man hadn't been his favorite member of the tribe. If he refused to let Johanna help, he would look ungracious in front of the Chief and other leaders. He couldn't afford to do that. He knew he could pay for it later. The medicine man was rumored to favor all-out war with the whites. If that day came, he knew he would be top of his list of men to kill.

Scott beckoned the girls over and introduced them to the leaders hoping Becky would keep a civil tongue in her head. To his surprise, she was as charming as Johanna. The Chief welcomed them to his village which was comprised of a number of dome-shaped dwellings. The Chief pointed to one where Winona was resting.

CHAPTER 17

*B*ecky had to bend her head to go inside the building Scott called a wickiup, but once she was in, she found she had sufficient room to stand and move about. The dwelling, although small, was clean and tidy. A woman lay on fur blankets in one corner, her skin gleaming with sweat, a feverish look in her eyes. She hoped her sister would be able to help. She didn't like the way the medicine man had stared at them, his hatred reverberating off him in waves. He reminded her of Mr. Price for all the wrong reasons.

Johanna moved toward the young woman who shrank back from her. Scott moved forward to translate.

"Winona, my sister, this is my friend. She is a medicine woman among her people. She has strong medicine. We hope it will make you better."

Winona looked to her husband who nodded before she smiled back weakly at him.

"Thank you, my brother, for trying to help. I think it is too late. Please look out for my husband and my family. Life is difficult for us now. More so than when you left." The talking left her exhausted.

"You are tiring her out, Captain Jones. Will she let me examine her?" Johanna asked.

"Yes, she will. I will turn my back but cannot leave as you need an interpreter."

Johanna worked quickly. There was no rash but a high fever. Her twin asked a couple of questions which Scott then asked Winona's husband and translated back to Johanna. Winona had fallen asleep again.

"Yes, they had visitors recently from a wagon train. She was playing with her children by the river. Her children got sick but they have both recovered. What is it?"

"I think it is something similar to what Ma had. I don't think it is cholera, although I can't be sure. Can you bring her to the river to bathe her like we did for the others?" Johanna asked. Scott nodded. Johanna looked back at the patient. " We need boiled water. I want to rub her down with mint tea just as we did with my mother. Do the Indians have salt? Our doctor at home recommended drinking salted water when anyone fell ill."

CHAPTER 18

*D*espite Johanna speaking quickly, Scott listened carefully. He was desperate. The tense atmosphere in the camp spoke volumes. The braves were restless, some didn't like the white women being here. If Winona didn't recover, he was extremely worried about their reaction. It wouldn't matter to the medicine man that Johanna had done her best. He would make out another Indian had died at the hands of a white person.

He spoke rapidly to Winona's husband before they left to speak to the Chief. As he suspected, the medicine man argued against the bathing insisting it would kill her. He listened as Paco argued back. He didn't get involved. This wasn't his decision to make.

"You say this woman helped many others in your train?" Paco asked.

"Yes, she did. But that does not guarantee anything, my brother. Your wife could still die."

"I know but she is not getting better. I think she will die." Paco's voice cracked. He looked away, regaining his composure. "Maybe this way she can be saved."

It was soon settled. Winona's husband carried his wife to the river where he bathed her. He did exactly what Johanna told him to do. Becky helped Johanna bathe the woman and then Paco carried her back to their home. The men left the women to dry Winona who was now sleeping.

Johanna needed water so Becky offered to get it for her. She came out of the wickiup to find Scott and Paco waiting for them. As always, her heart leapt with pleasure being so near to Scott despite the circumstances.

"My brother thanks you for making his wife better. He said you and Johanna are golden visions," Scott said.

Becky smiled at Paco. "Thank you."

"You love my brother, yes?"

She didn't know what shocked her more. The fact he spoke English or what he said about her loving Scott. Flustered, she turned to go back into the lodge totally forgetting about the water.

"I no mean to make you go red," Paco apologized putting his hand on her arm. "I'm sorry."

She smiled at him showing him she knew he didn't mean any offense. With a quick glance at Scott, she saw he was ignoring her. Obviously, he didn't share her feelings. She nodded to Paco before returning to the lodge.

"David said Captain Jones is going to show him some horses later. I think we will be returning to our camp tomorrow, the next day at the latest. I think she will get better." Johanna checked Winona's fever as she spoke.

"I hope so. She seems a nice lady. I like her husband, Paco."

"He is very close to Captain Jones. David said they are like brothers."

"Yes. I see that," Becky replied automatically, her thoughts all confused by Paco's remark. She'd thought she was hiding her feelings really well but obviously not.

"Becky, what is it? Something happen outside?"

"Paco asked if I was in love with Scott."

Johanna smiled. "Well, it's obvious so I guess not only we can see it. Do you mind?"

"Scott ignored me. He wouldn't even look at me. He doesn't feel the same, yet I can't understand why. When we are alone, it's as if I was the only girl in the whole world. But now..." Becky could have stamped her foot in frustration. "Why does life have to be so complicated? If I was a man, I could just ask him to marry me."

"If you lived in our world you could ask him to share your blanket."

Startled both girls gasped. They hadn't felt or seen Paco come in.

"You speak good English. Why do you pretend not to?" Becky demanded.

"It is good soldiers and white men not know I understand." Paco said shrugging his shoulders and grinning. "They speak freely."

"What were you saying about Captain Jones?" Johanna asked. Becky guessed her sister was giving her time to calm her temper.

"My brother has what you call demons. He has seen much sorrow and his heart is in pain. I think you are the woman to fix it but you must have patience."

Becky stared at him wondering what Scott had been through. His wife had died but how? They must have been madly in love and Scott was devastated by her death. That would certainly explain a few things.

"That will be the day. Becky wasn't born with a patient bone in her body," Johanna remarked not unkindly. She was simply stating the truth.

"I think we can all find patience if what we want is worth it," Paco said looked directly at Becky.

"Can you keep him safe, Paco? I know there is something he is planning and he won't tell me the details. Can you watch out for him?" Becky pleaded.

"I will try. I will also ask our sprits to watch for him. He is good man. He is good match for you and you for him. You are strong woman. I can see this in your eyes. And in your clothes," he added, his grin showing he understood Becky had taken a stand in the white man's world by dressing as she did.

CHAPTER 19

*L*ater, Johanna asked Becky to make some mint tea. She needed water.

"Can you please get some water for me?" Becky asked a young boy whom she took to be Winona's son. "I need to make some tea for Winona."

Paco translated for her. The young boy picked up two baskets and headed toward the exit of the wickiup.

"Wait please, I said water." She looked to Paco who nodded, his expression confused.

"He is going to get you water."

"In a basket?" Becky asked disbelievingly.

Paco looked from her to the basket and back with a frown on his face. "What else would he carry water in?"

Becky was out of her depth. She looked around for Scott. By the time they brought the basket back, the water would have leaked out.

She waved Scott over to them. His concerned expression made her feel uncomfortable but then she had no choice she needed water.

"I need some water but I don't think Paco understands. He is sending his son out with a basket not a bucket."

Scott laughed causing Becky's temper to rise. "What is so funny?"

"Shoshone use baskets to carry water. It won't leak."

Becky stared at him not bothering to hide her disbelief. He spoke rapidly to Paco in their own language and soon he and his son were laughing too. The boy hid his smile at the look of displeasure on Becky's face.

"We should not laugh. It is small mistake. We use baskets to carry everything from the big things to small pine nuts. Our women make good ones. Nothing drops."

He must have seen he hadn't convinced her. "When you are finished, I will show you."

"Thank you," Becky answered before turning back to find out what else she could do to help Johanna.

CHAPTER 20

Sometime later after Winona had been sleeping for a while, Becky took a walk outside. Paco spotted her leaving the wickiup and motioned her to follow him. He led her over to where some of the women were working. He introduced her. The women smiled shyly but none of them spoke English. She watched them work for a while marveling at their skill in turning rushes into weaved baskets.

When Paco returned for her, one of the Indian women handed her a finished one.

"It is for you. A gift."

Becky smiled and bowed to the Indian lady causing much bowing in return and laughter.

"Your people are very nice."

"What did you expect? That they would eat you for dinner?"

Becky didn't look him in the face. She was too ashamed for judging all Indians based on stupid stories she had read back in Virgil.

* * *

SOMETIME LATER, there was a commotion outside in the camp. Johanna was sleeping so Becky went outside to see what was going on. One of the Indians Paco had left with the horses was dragging someone behind him. She strained to see who it was. Almanzo—what was he doing here? She pushed through the Indians blocking her way. "Let me through. Get out of the way."

Despite most of the braves being bigger than her, they let her pass. She ran toward Almanzo.

"Almanzo. Are you okay? What have you done to him?" She rounded on the Indian holding on to the end of the rope that was bound around the boy's hands. "Let him go you heathen. What sort of man ties up a ten-year-old boy and drags him around?"

"Becky, stop."

"I will not stop. Scott, make them release Almanzo. Can't you see he needs help?"

"He needs a drink and a rest. Otherwise, he is fine, aren't you boy?" Scott addressed the child.

Almanzo nodded, the fear in his eyes leaving him unable to speak.

"What are you doing here?" Becky asked him.

"Let the boy drink and rest before you interrogate him," Scott commanded before he spoke to the Indian who cut Almanzo free but not before making it obvious he wanted to keep him prisoner.

Becky gave the boy some water to drink. While he was doing that, she washed his hands and then his face. He was burnt. Her anger rising, she turned on the Indian and gave him a piece of her mind. Despite not understanding English, the braves knew she was very angry from her tone and body language.

"You just made half my men fall in love with you. He Who Runs will have competition," Paco said coming toward her.

She turned on him and was about to chew him out, too, when he waved a piece of cloth at her.

"I couldn't find white. Stop shouting." Seeing her facial expression, Paco pleaded. "Please. See why boy come? Is there problem at your camp?"

Becky was mortified. She hadn't stopped to think that's why Almanzo had come to find them. Ma, Pa, Stephen, Eva and the others. Were they okay?

"Why you come here?" Paco asked Almanzo.

"To find Jo. I protect her."

Becky saw Paco hide his smile. She looked back at Almanzo. He looked so much younger than ten.

"Oh, sweetheart, Johanna is fine. You nearly got

yourself killed."

"He jumped me." Almanzo pointed at the Indian holding the rope used to tie him up. "Otherwise, I could have fought him."

"And the rest? You were brave but foolish," Paco gestured to one of the younger braves surrounding them. "Walking Tall will bring you to river to wash. Then he will show you some tricks to keep you safe."

At the word safe, Almanzo went white. Becky hastened to reassure him.

"Paco means in future. We are safe here."

The relief in Almanzo's eyes almost brought Becky to tears. She gave the boy a quick hug. "Johanna and I are in that wickiup. You are not allowed inside but get Paco to tell us if you need us. Go on with Paco's son. You will be fine."

Almanzo nodded rubbing at the chaffing on his arms. The ropes had been tied a little too tightly. Becky glared at the Indian holding the rope wishing she could tie him up and drag him along to show him what it felt like.

"Thoughts like that will not help friendship with my people," Paco whispered beside her. She stared at him in shock.

"How did you know what I was thinking?"

"You wear heart in your eyes. You are easy to read," Paco said smiling at her. Then he was gone.

CHAPTER 21

They stayed two nights, the girls taking turns to bathe Winona. Rick Hughes had promised to keep the rest of the travelers on track so they wouldn't lose too many miles. He was worried about the weather turning harsh. Hughes was steady and sensible. The group would be safe in his hands. Scott left David and Almanzo sitting at the fire outside the wickiup where Johanna and Becky were. He needed to speak to the Chief and he knew the Indians wouldn't speak freely in front of his friends regardless of the fact that the white men didn't understand their language.

Scott sat cross-legged at the fire with the Chief and his advisors ignoring the glares the medicine man sent in his direction. It was clear things were becoming more difficult. The young braves and those with a lust for fighting were becoming difficult to restrain. They were fed up with white people walking freely over their lands. They didn't seem to care they were moving on to live in another part of the country. Their wagons were scaring off the animals and destroying the grass and plants. Scott couldn't help but sympathize with his Indian brothers. If his wife and children were starving, he may feel the same. But it wasn't the time to show sympathy or weakness. He had to get everyone safe to Oregon and he needed the tribe to help him do that.

PACO HAD TOLD the tribe Mitchell was around and they were angry. Scott listened to their rants for a while before he gave the same warning to the Chief as he had given to Paco. It was important they let Scott deal with Mitchell. A white man killing another white man would not cause the same repercussions as if it had been an Indian. The Chief was annoyed.

"I can hold my people back from killing innocent white people but that man was responsible for killing the mothers, brothers and sisters of my braves. I cannot ask them not to take revenge."

"You must." Silence greeted Scott's remark. "You know I speak out of love for your people, not out of concern for myself. The army will not care that Mitchell killed so many of your people. They will see it as justification for another attack."

Silence again. Then the Chief finally spoke.

"I will speak to my braves but I will not order them to keep away from the black hearted devil. Instead, I will tell them the reason why you want to be the one to kill him. But if he should meet a natural or white man death we cannot be blamed."

He smiled, understanding the Chief's reasoning. His braves could use Mitchell's tricks against him. If they hanged him it would seem like the white man administered justice. Hanging was not a method of killing favored by the Indians. If the Indians pretended it was white men who killed Mitchell, there would be no repercussions. It was a good compromise.

CHAPTER 22

*E*arly the next morning, Scott sent Almanzo off to spend time with Walking Tall, Paco's son. He wanted to speak to David in private. They sat outside the wickiup where Johanna and Becky were staying.

After he had finished explaining what had been discussed with the Chief, he waited for David's reaction. It took a while. David was obviously uncomfortable.

"I understand the need for revenge. I could have killed my own father more times than I care to admit but I still think you are wrong. If you kill this man you will make yourself no better than he is. Either capture him and let the authorities deal with him, or forget about him." Although David spoke quietly, there was no denying his belief in what he said.

He didn't reply. He couldn't make David understand

that after years of living with Indians, he was more accustomed to their ways than the white man's.

"Are your horses here?"

He smiled. He had forgotten about them. "Yes, let me take you to see them. Paco's son has been minding them for me. He will take us. Later when his chores are finished."

He whistled to a young teenager who ran over to them. The boy couldn't wait to show him, talking excitedly about the foals who were growing up as majestic as their father. Almanzo followed in his wake.

"I think someone has a real case of hero worship." David indicated Almanzo to Scott.

"Walking Tall is a good role model. He can teach him a lot."

By MID-MORNING, Winona's temperature had broken. Becky came out to tell Paco. She also told him not to get his hopes by warning him Winona may get ill again. Paco picked up Becky and twirled her around making her laugh loudly. Scott's gut twisted at her natural reaction, seeing his brother-in-law with the girl he loved made him question his intentions. What if David was right? Was he wrong not to forget Mitchell and enjoy a future with this beautiful woman?

Then Paco's younger son, walked up to say thank you to Becky for saving his mother. Scott's throat tightened as he looked at the boy who had been born the same summer as his son. Mitchell had stolen that future away from him. He had to pay.

BECKY ENJOYED her time at the camp. She had always been curious but if she had been pushed to be honest, also a little afraid of Indians. But two nights among them and she saw they were just like the people in the wagon train. There were nice Indians, grumpy ones and ones that were scary. Winona and her husband were very much in love and their children were so well behaved. She had caught the look of pain on Scott's face when he saw Paco's young son. Had he been in love with Winona but she chose Paco over him? He'd said he would explain but he seemed in no hurry.

Paco came over to speak to her. "You remind me of an old Shoshone warrior."

"I remind you of a boy. Thank you so much." Her sarcasm seemed to amuse him.

"This woman's name was Sacagawea. When she was ten summers she was kidnapped by another tribe who sold her into slavery. Her white owner married her and they had children together."

"So why do I remind you of her?" Becky asked mystified.

"She helped the first white men over the Rockies. She wasn't afraid of anything. Legend has it, she kept the men fed, and also, provided them with horses by introducing them to her brother who had become a Shoshone chief in her absence. It is a big compliment. She is seen as a very brave woman."

"So Indians let women lead expeditions. And they say your people are the savages."

Scott laughed. "She didn't lead the expedition, although, I concede, she was allowed to go. Indians treat their women as being important. They have a lot of rights and freedom, but women are not warriors nor do they become chiefs."

Becky stuck her tongue out at Scott for teasing her, making Paco laugh.

CHAPTER 23

Sometime later, Paco came for Becky again. Telling her to bring Johanna with her, he directed them over to a group of women who were all chattering excitedly.

"Take a seat," he said to Becky.

"Why?" Becky asked, her voice higher than normal due to her nervousness.

"They want to thank you for looking after Winona. It is a great honor to have the leather sewn while on your feet. Usually, only chiefs or brave warriors get this honor."

"Please thank them but there is no need," she fidgeted.

"My sister can't sit still for long, Paco," Johanna said earning a glare from Becky.

"Yes, she is like bear who sits on bees' home. Always moving," Paco said mimicking Becky.

Johanna and Paco laughed as Becky made a face. Despite what she said, she was enjoying the feel of the tanned leather against her feet. The fact that they were made especially for her, would make them more comfortable than her current shoes. Sitting still while they sewed the leather pieces together with sinew wasn't too high a price to pay for comfort.

The moccasins were so comfortable she insisted Johanna get a pair too.

"Your dress will cover them up but they are really comfortable. Try it."

Johanna took a seat while the ladies fussed over her.

Walking Tall came over with Almanzo trailing him.

"You enjoying yourself?" Becky asked the youngster.

"It's amazing. Tall here has been teaching me lots of things."

"Tall?"

"His real name is too long so I shortened it. He calls me Al."

Becky smiled at the Indian boy who returned her smile shyly.

"Is everyone treating you all right?" she asked in a lower voice even though Paco's son didn't speak much English.

"More or less. The medicine man isn't too happy,"

Almanzo added. "Some of his friends keep glaring at me, but I just ignore them."

"I think that might be Johanna's fault. The medicine man couldn't cure Winona and now Johanna has, he looks bad. Silly really as we could learn a lot from each other, but some people can be funny."

"Like my pa," Almanzo whispered. "How could he hate all these people? They are just the same as us. Well, if they had white skins, I mean." Almanzo blushed.

She reached over and ruffled his hair. "You are turning out to be a lovely boy. Johanna and Rick will be so proud of you."

Almanzo beamed. "Can I go now? It's not time to go home yet, is it?"

"No, not yet but soon."

Becky watched the boy as he ran off with his Indian friend. If Mr. Price could see him now, he would probably drop dead from apoplexy. She smiled.

"You seem happy. Why?" Johanna asked.

"Just thinking it's funny how life turns out. You couldn't imagine meeting anyone who hates Indians much more than Mr. Price, yet his son has a new best friend. If he was here, he would have a fit."

"Becky, if he was still part of the train, Almanzo wouldn't have had this opportunity. Sometimes things do happen for a reason."

CHAPTER 24

 ecky made her way back toward Winona's wickiup. Hopefully the woman would be able to walk around a bit today. Johanna was fretting she would have a relapse and wanted to stay another day. But Scott was anxious to get back to their group to see how they had fared on their continuing journey. Oregon was still some miles away.

Paco was visiting his wife who seemed much better. "I take my brother to see his horses again. Do you want come?"

She wanted to go but it would mean leaving Johanna alone. She couldn't do that. "I must stay with my sister, but thank you."

"Becky, go with Paco. I am safe here. Nobody comes into the lodge. You won't be long, will you?"

"We come back quick." He nodded to his wife.

"Nobody will interrupt my wife's peace. I leave guard just in case."

"Are you sure, Johanna? Rick will kill me if he finds out."

"Nobody is going to tell him or Pa. Go on. I know how much you love horses."

She gave her sister an impulsive hug. "Thank you," she said before she followed Paco outside. He mounted a horse and offered her his hand to pull her up behind him. She had no option but to hold her hands around his middle, the closeness making her eyes water with his scent. She wondered what Paco used to smell so bad.

"My brother would say no if I asked to bring you. I will ask forgiveness instead."

Becky laughed. Paco knew Scott so well. "You must teach me how to get my own way with Scott."

"My brother like strong woman."

"But Indian women are not strong-minded, are they? I thought they were quite docile."

"I do not understand."

"I thought they say yes to men a lot," Becky explained.

"Ha. Only when men suggest something they want to do. If Indian woman no want to do something, would be easier to move mountain than make her say yes. Women in charge of lots of things in Indian village. The children, the lodge. If man not treat her right, Indian woman will throw man out of lodge. Not good."

She couldn't believe that. A white man could do whatever he liked to his wife, and she wouldn't have the right to stop him going into his own house. The differences in tradition and culture were fascinating. How hard it must have been for Scott to try to live in both worlds.

* * *

PACO HAD BEEN RIGHT about his brother not wanting her there. Scott had almost pulled her off the horse demanding to know what she'd been thinking coming out here alone with Paco.

"I knew he wouldn't hurt me," she said, rubbing her arm where he had grabbed it.

"I am not worried about him hurting you. What would have happened to him if a man like Price saw an Indian with a white girl on the back of his horse? Honestly, Becky, do you ever engage your brain?"

"I didn't think," she murmured quietly as shame overwhelmed her.

"No, you never do."

"That's not fair." But she was speaking to his back.

She twirled around when she heard Paco laughing behind her. Putting her hands on her waist, she took her temper out on him. After all, it had been his idea to come, and Scott hadn't said a word to him. "What is so funny?"

"My brother is like a bear with a sore...paw. He was the same when..." He stopped speaking obviously deciding he shouldn't tell the rest of that story. It infuriated Becky even more.

"He was like that when..." she prompted.

Paco remained stone faced. "I have said too much already. Come see horses."

"No. Why won't anyone tell me? Scott won't say anything and now you stop talking too."

"It is his story. Let him tell you in his own time. Now come, see the horses."

The stubborn set of Paco's chin told her she wouldn't get anything more out of him. She had no choice but to follow him.

CHAPTER 25

The sight of the animals soon put her bad mood behind her. They were fabulous creatures, running free.

"Magnificent, aren't they?" Scott came up beside her, his gazed centered on the animals, a look of adoration on his face.

"Yes." Becky managed to stammer after a couple of seconds. "Who owns them?" She asked, desperate to keep Scott talking.

"Paco and I do. We caught some wild horses some years back. We have been breeding them since," he said, looking so proud, you would think he had given birth to them himself.

She knew from seeing how he treated animals how much he loved them. But his feelings for these horses went deeper than that.

"They are very intelligent animals. If you listen to what they tell you, you will learn a lot."

"How can I listen to a horse? They don't talk?"

"They communicate just like we do although they do not use words. But they will tell us when they are happy or sad, when danger is lurking, whether the weather is changing. All sorts of things."

Becky wasn't sure what to say. She had never heard of anyone communicating with a horse. The men on the wagon trail sometimes spoke to their horses but rarely went further than telling them to speed up or slow down.

"But how do you know they are yours? They are not marked or in pens," she asked.

"Like this."

Scott gave a low whistle. Becky watched in awe as two of the horses pinned their ears back as if listening. Her mouth hung open as they galloped over to Scott nudging him with their heads.

"You tamed them?"

"They are still wild at heart but they respond to kindness. Paco is wonderful with horses. He taught me everything I know."

Paco wandered over just in time to hear Scott's remark.

"He Who Runs is being kind. He was born knowing how to speak to animals. They trust him. See."

Becky watched as a beautiful black stallion made its way over to Scott. The horse stamped and blew air out his nostrils as if to remind them he was the boss. Eventually, he too nudged Scott's shoulder as if looking for recognition.

"Do you want to come for a ride?" Scott asked her.

"On him?" she replied slightly terrified but exhilarated at the same time. "But he hasn't got a saddle."

"Paco's horse didn't have one and you managed."

Becky bit her lip. Was that a touch of jealousy in his tone? She wasn't about to give up a chance to hold him close.

"Yes, please."

"Okay, move closer so he can smell you. Then I will mount and help you up behind me."

Becky nodded, moving closer to the horse who tried to nibble her hair. She giggled at the sensation but her breath left her body when Scott took her hand and pulled her up behind him. She held on tightly to his body, savoring his scent. She put her arms around his waist and her head against his shoulder as he urged the horse to go faster and faster. It was the most incredible ride but all too soon it was over. When he sensed her disappointment, he explained quietly,

"We can't go far. It's time to get back to camp. We have to collect your sister too."

She'd forgotten all about Johanna and everything

else. For that brief moment, it had only been her and Scott. Feeling guilty, she didn't plead for more time. Instead, she allowed him to help her down.

"Thank you for taking me. He is truly magnificent. How do you keep them safe? I mean when you are not around."

"Walking Tall, Paco and the Indians look out for them but horses are very intelligent. They have lived on this land longer than us. It is only when they wish to share our lives, they let us tame them."

She looked from him to the horse and back again. He really believed everything he said.

"What are you planning to do with them?" she asked softly wanting him to confide his plans for the future. But her plan was thwarted when Paco spoke.

"You wish to ride back with me to camp?" Paco asked.

Much as she was tempted to make Scott jealous, she didn't think her stomach could handle being so close to the Indian.

"I will ride with David, but thank you."

"You ride with me. I am responsible for you," Scott replied.

Although she was tempted to pull him up for telling her what to do, she was delighted he insisted she ride with him. This time, she nuzzled his neck as they rode behind the others.

'Becky, cut that out."

"Why, don't you like it?"

"Becky, you are so…"

"Wild and exciting?" she murmured, licking the side of his ear. With an exclamation, he jumped down from the horse pulling her after him. He wrapped his arms around her and kissed her. She moved closer to his body, wishing they could stay here forever, in each other's arms.

"You are a vixen," he whispered when they came up for air.

"You shouldn't be so tempting," she responded back, her tongue wetting her lips drawing his gaze and a groan.

"I swear you would tempt a saint. We have to get back."

"I love you, Scott."

He stilled at her words, his arms falling to his side.

"Becky, you can't. I'm sorry. I knew you were innocent and I still allowed you to seduce me."

"I know you love me. People don't kiss like that when they aren't in love."

He groaned but this time not with passion.

"I forget you are so young and inexperienced. You have no idea what you are talking about. What's between us is just…well, it's not love."

"You don't mean that. I know you don't. You care for

me. You are just too… too chicken to admit it," she said glaring at him.

"Let's get back. They will be worried."

He helped her up on the horse once more, but this time, she held on to his back only because she had to. Tears ran down her face but she didn't make a sound. She wasn't about to let him know how much he'd humiliated her.

CHAPTER 26

*J*ohanna looked up as Paco's young son came inside the wickiup.

"Father and your friends are back. You go now?"

"Little Bear!" Winona admonished weakly.

"We go now," Johanna smiled at the boy. She didn't think he was being rude, just simply asking a question. She was keen to get back to Rick anyway. She had missed him. While she was happy to help the Indians, she wasn't comfortable here. Too many of them viewed her with suspicion, a few with downright hatred like the medicine man. Winona was getting better. With luck, she would completely recover. She knew it was a lot of luck as she really had no idea what illness Winona had and whether it was the cold-water bath or the mint tea, or most likely, a combination of both that had helped.

She walked outside to watch as the others rode in. Becky looked strained as did Captain Jones. Something must have happened between them. It didn't take a genius to work out they'd had a disagreement. Becky looked as if she had been crying but her sister wouldn't appreciate her bringing anyone's attention to that fact.

She hoped Becky hadn't done something impulsive. She would have to wait until later to find out, now was not the time. She held her breath as she was embraced by a number of Indians. She bowed to the Chief who thanked her again for coming. He told her she was welcome on his land whenever she felt like visiting. She said thank you, despite knowing that once they reached Oregon she would never return. If Rick wanted to see his grandmother back East he could go alone. She'd had enough of traveling to last her a lifetime.

AS THEY SAID GOODBYE, Winona presented them with some cured hides. She said something to Captain Jones who translated.

"She says it will keep you warm on your travel in the big hills," he explained as they took their leave. Johanna took Becky's hand as they walked behind Captain Jones, David, and Paco. Almanzo and Walking Tall followed behind the women leading Almanzo's horse.

Their horses were where they had left them. A rapid conversation transpired between Captain Jones and the Indians who had been left to mind their horses. Becky asked David what it was about, but he said he didn't know. Somehow, Johanna knew he was lying and it made her uneasy. David Clarke was one of the most honest men she knew. If he didn't want them to know something, it could only mean trouble. Her need to get back to Rick intensified. He would be worried sick about Almanzo. She wanted to leave now but that would be rude. Instead, she moved from one foot to the other as Captain Jones seemed to take forever to say goodbye to Paco.

"My son will miss you, Al," Paco said to Almanzo.

"Me too, Mr. Paco," Almanzo said. "He's my first Indian friend."

The adults exchanged smiles.

"Miss Johanna, you will always be welcome in my home. You and feisty lady." Paco winked at Becky. Becky's mouth hung open as David and Johanna laughed. Paco turned back toward his home.

"Didn't take him long to get to know you Becky," David commented, rather bravely thought Johanna. Becky looked like she was fit to kill someone.

"Come on, let's get back. Ma will be worried," Johanna said.

They spurred their horses faster, eager now to see their loved ones.

CHAPTER 27

*R*ick and their wagon train had made good progress. They were surrounded by people, their horses taken away to be rubbed down and watered.

"I am so glad you came back, Jo, we missed you." Carrie wouldn't let her hand go. "Almanzo, too, but Uncle Rick said he was in a lot of trouble."

"I missed you too, darling, but I had to help Captain Jones' friend. Almanzo knows he shouldn't have run off like that and scared everyone but he wanted to find me. He thought I needed protection."

"What was it like in the Indian camp? Where they all really scary?" Sarah asked.

"Indians don't scare me none," Almanzo answered.

"I wasn't talking to you," Sarah snapped, causing Rick to give Johanna a meaningful look. She couldn't wait to spend time alone with her fiancé, but first the children needed her.

"The Indians are just the same as us. They have families and they worry about each other. They go hunting for food...well, at least, the men and boys do. The women and girls stay in the village looking after the old people, the babies and taking care of the chores.

"So it's no better being an Indian girl than a white one?" Sarah's disgust was barely hidden. "We still get to do all the chores?"

Johanna laughed at the disappointment on the young girls face. "Yes, darling, I am sorry but it's true. If anything, the female Indians work harder than we do. They do all sorts of things we don't."

"Like what?"

Johanna's mind went blank. She looked to Rick for help.

"Come on, let's leave Jo to have some sleep. She looks rather tired," Rick said ushering the girls away. "I am guessing she stayed up all night over the last two nights minding her patient."

"Poor Jo, you do look old and tired."

Johanna burst out laughing. "Less of the old, thank you, Carrie. But I am tired so why don't you come to see me later. When I have had a rest."

"They can see you tomorrow. It's my turn to talk to you later," Rick's insistent tone worried her.

"Do you have something to tell me?" she asked.

"Well, talking is overrated but I can think of something to do." He gave her a meaningful look.

"Look, Sarah, Jo is going all red. See, even her ears are turning redder," Carrie shouted out.

Johanna got more embarrassed. She quickly said goodbye and walked back to her tent, the sound of the children's laughter ringing in her ears. Her ma was smiling too.

"Ma, I am really sorry but I think I will fall asleep standing up."

"You get to bed, girl. Becky is already snoring. I will keep dinner for you. I am so proud of you. I am fit to burst."

Johanna smiled before she went into the tent she shared with Becky. She lay down wondering how her patient was getting on. Was there any more sickness among her new friends? She soon fell fast asleep.

RICK CAUGHT up with Almanzo just as the boy was finished telling Stephen all about his adventure.

"Stephen, can I have a word with Almanzo alone, please."

"Yes, sir, see you," Stephen said quickly running away.

Almanzo stood with his hands behind his back, his eyes on the floor. Rick bent down to his level and gently made him look at him. "I am very happy to see you came back safely, Almanzo."

"Thank you, Rick."

"You know you shouldn't have gone without telling me or another adult?"

"Yes, sir, but you wouldn't have let me go."

Rick had to hide a smile at the honesty of the reply." Would you do it again?"

Almanzo keep quiet for too long.

"Almanzo?"

"Honestly, sir, yes, I would if I thought you were going to stop me. I know that ain't what you want to hear but I had the best time. I made new friends. The Indians are super nice, not a bit like what my pa said. I learned a lot."

"That's good, son, and I am very glad but please don't go without telling me next time. I don't need more grey hair."

Almanzo nodded. He stood waiting in silence. When Rick didn't say anything, he looked up, the fear in his eyes making Rick want to find Mr. Price and thump him.

"You going to whip me now?" Almanzo eventually whispered.

'Why on earth would I do that?"

"'Cause I ran off. My pa, he used to whip me for all sorts of stuff."

"No, son. I won't be doing that. I don't agree with whipping children. If you do something wrong, I will tell you and together we will decide on your punishment."

"Really?" Almanzo's eyes highlighted his disbelief.

"Yes, really. So starting now, what do you think is a fair punishment for going off alone to the camp?"

"Dunno."

"I don't know is the correct answer. Jo tells me you are behind with your schooling."

"Pa never let me go," Almanzo said defensively.

"Education is very important, Almanzo. You need to read and write properly. So tonight, you can show me how well you can read. Every night, you will read for at least fifteen minutes."

"Ah shucks. Couldn't you whip me instead?"

CHAPTER 28

The days passed as they continued their travels. Becky found the journey was beyond monotonous with the same scenery around them. Everyone, including Ma who was usually so good-tempered, was snappy and ill-tempered. Becky was quieter than usual, not that anyone noticed. She hadn't seen Scott alone for a while.

Tension filled the air and it wasn't solely caused by couples fighting or parents snapping at children. It had been some days since they'd last found water and their supplies were worryingly low. They had rationed themselves to a cup a day each. It wasn't enough, especially as the air was dusty from the sand on the roads. The cattle weren't faring much better. The best grass had been eaten by the animals from the trains ahead of them leaving sparse vegetation in their midst.

"Look, that's a river bed, isn't it?" someone shouted out. She thought it might be Mr. Bradley, but she couldn't be sure.

"Let's go check it out. Seems like it might be as there is grass beside it. The cattle will be happy," Pa commented, a smile back on his face.

"Shouldn't we wait for Captain Jones and Rick to get back?"

"No, they will see us. Come on, you want a drink, don't you?"

A drink? She wanted to take a bath in nice, cool, refreshing water. She shook the thoughts out of her head and concentrated on the task at hand. It wasn't a steep slope but she didn't want any accidents with the wagon now.

When they got to the river bed, they were severely disappointed.

"Where did the water all go?' Julia's voice trembled as the tears streamed down her face. "Those look like muddy puddles not a big river."

Johanna bent down to give the little girl a hug. "The water must have dried into the ground. We will find some. You go play with Carrie, she can show you her books."

She knew Julia didn't believe Johanna but she went with Carrie and Sarah anyway. She put the brake on the wagon and jumped down.

Grabbing a shovel, she turned to her twin. "So where do you think the water is?"

"How do I know. We just have to dig until we find it."

Taken aback by Johanna's uncharacteristic terseness, she decided to say nothing and start digging. They dug for a while before the men came and relieved them. Thankfully, they did as they didn't hit water until the hole was four or five feet down.

"We'll have to sieve it as it's so sandy. It will do until we find a better supply."

"Maybe Captain Jones will have found a spring. And some meat. Wouldn't that be fantastic?"

"Not asking for much are you, Becky?" Johanna said grinning, this time no trace of anger in her tone. "Sorry for biting your head off earlier."

"It's okay. I'm glad to see I am not the only one fed up with all this." Becky waved around her. "I can't wait until we are in a real town."

"In a proper house that doesn't move."

"And has a well and a pump and a bath."

The sisters giggled as their list became more demanding. By the time Scott and Rick had returned, they were nearly hysterical. Both men looked at each other as if wondering whether the women were going mad from lack of water or too much sun.

"Did you find water?"

"Yes, but it is too far away for the wagons to get there tonight. We will reach it late afternoon at the earliest."

Becky groaned.

"But we brought you back a present," Rick handed his canteen to Johanna. She took a mouthful and then another one. "Go on, drink. We brought enough for everyone to have at least a cup."

Scott handed his canteen to Becky, her skin tingling at his touch. He looked tired, his eyes clouded with pain. She longed to say something to ease his pain but what? She had bared her soul and he'd told her they had no future. He'd made his mind up. She had to live with that. The water lost its attraction. She couldn't stand here close to him without being able to touch or embrace him like Johanna had done with Rick. She moved away, using the excuse of having to find her pa to give him the fresh water.

DAVID FOUND an actual stream a few miles away from the river bed. They forced themselves to travel to it knowing it would be better for both man and beast.

"I am not going another step. Not one single one."

"Okay, my darling, I will carry you." David picked Eva up and carried her the last few steps to the river.

"Isn't he so nice—oh my!" Ma started laughing as

David unceremoniously dumped his wife in the river. Eva screamed in shock before trying to turn David's joke back on him. She kicked as much water as she could in his direction but her skirts hampered her efforts. David laughed and teased her from the river bank. Johanna caught Becky's hand and pointed toward someone on the bank. Captain Jones snuck up behind David, picked him up and threw him into the river beside his wife. The children soon followed suit, jumping in after the adults. It was just the break everyone needed after the tedious travels of the previous few days.

Becky caught Scott's eye as he laughed at the antics in the water. She smiled thinking how relaxed he looked. He smiled back making her insides quiver but then he turned his back leaving her feeling bereft.

SCOTT WATCHED the people in the water. He had grown close to them over the journey. They'd been through so much together. If he married Becky, he could continue to live among these people. Raise a family with them as neighbors. Why couldn't he forget Mitchell?

CHAPTER 29

he roads over the mountain were extremely hilly and rough. They didn't cover as many miles as they had previously. The scenery was delightful and there was plenty of grass for the animals. They traveled about ten miles before meeting an Indian who showed them where to water the cattle. Johanna didn't recognize him from the camp but it was clear Captain Jones knew him. She watched as they greeted each other. It seemed friendly but she sensed he didn't know this man as well as he had known the previous group.

They were soon surrounded by a herd of horses and ponies. The children became very excited.

"Do you think they would let us ride them?" Stephen asked excitedly.

"I don't think so, Stephen. Those horses are wild and not suitable for riding unless you can ride bare back."

"I can ride without a saddle," Almanzo said, his eyes on Sarah.

"Really? Where did you learn to do that?" Sarah challenged him.

"It's easy. Anyone can do it. Look at that boy, he looks a lot younger than me."

The Indian boy looked to be about Carrie's age but he was in complete control of his horse. Rick laughed but quickly turned it into a choke as Johanna frowned at him.

"Almanzo, darling, the Indian boys are different from us," Johanna said gently. "They are taught to ride without saddles from a very young age. Don't try to be brave or heroic. We have had enough illness and injury to last a life time."

Almanzo didn't say a word but frowned, looking at the ground.

"Promise me you will not try to ride."

"Yes, ma'am, but…"

"But what, Almanzo?"

"Walking Tall showed me how to ride when I was at the camp. I'll be careful, I promise."

"Let him go, Jo, he has to learn and it looks like he made a good friend."

They watched as Almanzo and the Indian boy greeted each other like long lost brothers. Johanna's heart was in her mouth as Almanzo mounted a horse, but to her surprise, he handled it very well. He was growing up.

* * *

"Thank you for coming together tonight. We have to cross the river and the current, while not as fast as some, is unpredictable. My friend, Ahmik—his name means Beaver—will help us across. He knows this river better than anyone."

"Can you not do it, Captain Jones?"

"No, Mrs. Newland. Ahmik is the expert. He will guide the cattle too. He knows the easiest places for them to cross."

"Is his service expensive?"

"No, Mrs. Long. He would like some fresh meat for his family. I have taken care of it."

"Thank you, Captain Jones. When do we cross?"

"In the morning. It is too dangerous to attempt at night."

"Is there no way around the river?"

Milly's nervous tone had her husband, Stan, reaching for her hand.

"You will be fine, Milly, Johanna and Becky will travel with you. You ladies will cross first."

"I'm sorry Captain Jones but I can't travel with Milly. Well, not unless she wants to go over by canoe." Becky's smirk made him angry but he couldn't say anything. Not here in front of her pa.

"Becky, I don't think that is wise. It's not safe."

"Sure it is Ma. Beaver will take me. He promised."

"You spoke to Ahmik?"

Becky shook her head, her eyes looking beyond him. He knew who he would find without turning his head.

"Paco, what on earth are you doing this far away from your village?"

"I was bored and hungry. We tracked some deer near to you but they were scared away by the noise of your camp."

Paco smiled, but he knew better than to believe his brother's explanation. There was another reason for him being here.

"You told Becky she could go over in the canoe?" he asked, trying to keep his tone cool.

"Not exactly. I said I would paddle and she could travel with me if she wishes. She has a wild spirit. Let it fly free for a while. When she gets to Oregon they will make her dress like a woman again. Her life will be changed forever."

Paco spoke his native tongue so the others couldn't understand, but his brother's perception of Becky's situation impressed him. Was there nothing this man did not understand?

"Captain Jones, perhaps you could talk Becky out of

this nonsense?" Mrs. Thompson frowned at her daughter.

"She will be perfectly safe with Paco, Mrs. Thompson. He knows the river like the back of his hand."

Becky almost jumped up and down. He could see she wanted to but she restrained herself at the last minute. In some ways, she was still very much a child.

CHAPTER 30

*B*ecky stood to the side watching the interchange between Scott and the Indian who had piloted their wagons across the river. The Indian was agitated, but she couldn't make out what he was saying. She wasn't near enough to hear, not that it mattered as he wasn't speaking English. Had this something to do with Mitchell? She looked around for Paco but he had disappeared.

She made her way toward where Scott was talking, but instead of interrupting him, she waited until he had finished, and the Indian had moved away. Scott was in deep thought and didn't hear her approach.

"Something wrong?" she asked, wanting to put her arms around him and kiss away his worry.

"No."

"Try again and this time I might believe you." She

smiled to take the sting out of her words but she couldn't hide the concern in her eyes. "Trouble?"

"Might be but keep it to yourself."

"I am not that good of an actress. I wasn't the only one who saw you speaking to him. You will have to tell them something," she said, but when he didn't respond she continued, "why did Paco really come here today? It wasn't to canoe me over the river."

"I think that was part of it. Paco likes to have the last laugh on me."

Becky's heart jumped. He had admitted he was jealous. Hadn't he? She couldn't ask anymore as they heard people moving toward them.

He saw Johanna, Rick, and some of the children a little way off. "Did they hear?"

"I am sure they saw you but they couldn't hear you nor understand you," Becky reassured him but he had to face reality. "But they aren't stupid. You don't need to speak Indian to know that man was upset about something."

"The weather is turning bad."

"That is an excuse. No man, let alone an Indian, gets that agitated about some bad weather. Why don't you tell me the truth?"

He stayed silent.

She wasn't going to beg him to talk to her, she had a little more pride than that. But he needed to speak to someone. "Well, if you don't trust me, why not tell David? You should tell someone if only to let them protect the group."

"I trust you but I don't want to worry anyone. This is my problem."

She tried but failed to keep a grip on her anger. He wasn't thinking straight. "Look around you, Scott. This is not your problem. The Indian is concerned. The people who trusted you with their lives are worried. This stopped being your problem a long time ago, only you are too stubborn to admit it." Becky took a deep breath, "If Mitchell is coming after you, then he is coming after us. All of us. The Freemans, Bradleys, Longs, Newlands, Hugheses, Clarkes, Thompsons and me."

His head swung up, his eyes wide with alarm. He pulled her into his arms. Instead of being delighted, she was alarmed. Even more so when he held her too tight.

"You. He may try to hurt you. You must be more careful. Don't go anywhere alone. He knows what you look like."

"Scott, stop it. You're scaring me." Becky twisted a little so he loosened his grip. She reached up and kissed him on the lips but it was a kiss of reassurance not passion. "You must tell people. I will ask Pa to call a meeting tonight. You owe them honesty. You don't have to tell them the whole story. As much, or as little as you want. But they need to know a murderer is on our trail or waiting for us up ahead."

She kissed him quickly again before forcing herself to break away. He needed space to think.

HE WATCHED her walk back to the others. Was she only seventeen? At times, she acted much older. She was right. He had to warn the others. Mitchell had been spotted along with a group of renegades. He had already attacked one wagon train. Luckily, they managed to fight back. But according to his friend, there had been a lot more people in the train. Maybe that would put Mitchell off attacking again. He wished he could believe that.

CHAPTER 31

Scott stood looking at the people who had become his friends, his family, or at least that is how he saw them. He had a commercial duty to get them safely to Oregon but it was more than that. He wanted them to be happy and safe in their new home. They meant more to him than the money he was being paid. He looked from each face to the next, their expressions of trust mingled with anxiety or in some cases fear making him feel worse. His gaze stopped at Becky. She smiled at him, her eyes telling him she thought he was doing the right thing.

"I asked Mr. Thompson to call a meeting as we may have unwelcome company," Scott began.

The men eyed each other before looking back at Captain Jones. The women just stared as if not quite believing what their leader was saying.

"What type? Indians?"

"No, Mrs. Newland. This is a white man, maybe two of them."

"Who?"

"A man called Mitchell and perhaps a man we met previously, Harold's friend Bill."

"But what would they want with us?"

"It's not you they want, Mrs. Thompson. At least Mitchell doesn't. I am not sure what Bill is looking for."

"Could be revenge. You stopped him getting whatever Chapman promised him," Mrs. Thompson added.

"Knowing Harold and his big mouth, he probably said he would pay him a lot of money." Eva's disparaging tone made it quite clear what she thought of their ex traveler.

"Either way, we have to be on our guard. I do not want any of the women wandering anywhere alone. You all know how to use a gun, right?"

BECKY HELD her breath watching the reaction to his speech. Everyone nodded apart from Milly. Her hands were shaking. Becky took one and rubbed it, trying to ease her friend's mind. She was upset enough at the thought her baby may come early without having to worry about an attack.

"I don't understand. What would a white man want so badly he'd be willing to take on the whole train?"

Becky sighed, she guessed her pa wasn't trying to be racist but he made it sound like only Indians stole from white people.

"Some years ago, Mitchell attacked a wagon train. A couple of the survivors told the army that it was Indians who attacked them but their leader was a white man. The army didn't take much notice of that bit," Scott explained. "They only heard Indians and in retaliation they ambushed an Indian village and killed everyone they found. Including my wife and two children."

Becky nearly vomited. She'd known his wife was dead but murdered? And his children too. No wonder he was in so much pain. But why hadn't he told her in private? He should have known she would comfort him.

"I am sorry you lost your squaw but what's that got to do with Mitchell or us?"

"I lost my wife and children, Mr. Bradley."

Mr. Bradley turned pale at Captain Jones's tone.

"What Tom means is he is sorry for your loss, Captain Jones. We are a little confused as to the part Mitchell plays and why he is coming after us?"

"Thank you, Mrs. Long, for your sentiments. Mitchell is a land pirate. He wants any land deeds you already hold or the cash and other valuables you intend to exchange for the land. He led the attack against the two other wagon trains. He dressed up his men to look like Indians."

"They must have had some red skins, otherwise, people wouldn't believe that."

Mr. Newland's description caused Scotts eyes to flare with anger.

"Mr. Newland, I am sure it is easier for everyone to blame Indians rather than believe our own kind would turn against us," Becky said firmly.

Scott flashed her a grateful look.

"Mitchell hates me. Not only because I lived with the Indians as one of them, but because I consider my tribe my brothers. I owe them my life. When my family was massacred, I went after Mitchell. I tracked him down and turned him in to the authorities."

"I bet he didn't confess to the crimes."

"No, he didn't, Mr. Thompson, but living among the Indians gave me certain skills which helped him come to his senses."

"You tortured him into a confession?" Mrs. Newland's shock was reflected on the faces of everyone listening.

"Everyone, you got to remember this animal was the reason Scott's family was murdered, his friends, an entire village,"Becky stated. "And the innocent men, women and children on the wagon train. What would you do to the man who hurt us like that Pa?" Becky asked.

Mr. Thompson squirmed uncomfortably in his seat.

"I am sure you would skin someone alive if they touched your Sheila, Mr. Freeman, or your Gracie, Mr. Bradley." Both men looked as uncomfortable as her pa. Satisfied she looked at Scott to find him looking at her, his eyes full of sadness.

CHAPTER 32

*B*ecky gulped hard. What had she done wrong? She moved to go to him but one look was all it took to make her stay where she was.

"Contrary to Miss Thompson's overactive imagination, I didn't skin Mitchell alive or do anything else to him. Not physically. I simply reminded him we had witnesses to the wagon train massacres. I painted him mind pictures of what the Indians would do to him if I released him into their custody. Thankfully, he had read the same nonsensical articles most travelers use to form their opinions of my brothers."

"So Mitchell confessed. Why is he still alive?" Pa asked.

"I don't know. I was assured he would hang, yet we met him at Fort Hall."

"He was the man who was rude to me and Becky.

Horrible man with squinty, mean eyes and a scar on his face," Eva said, her face screwed up with distaste.

"Yes, Mrs. Clarke, that about sums up Mitchell."

"But if you met him in Fort Hall and he is after your blood, why hasn't he attacked you yet? And why would he want to hurt us?"

"He wants his revenge on me, Mr. Bradley, of that there is no doubt. But like most bullies, he is a coward at heart. He won't come after me alone. And he will need to pay those men he hires. He has learned his lesson. He won't leave any witnesses alive."

"So your actions have put our entire train in danger. The lives of my wife and children are at risk due to your...your past choices," Pa said, his tones and words making Becky cringe.

"Past choices? By that, if you are referring to losing your entire family in an Indian attack on a wagon train, being captured and worked as a slave all before you reach your sixth birthday then yes, I am guilty. The Shoshone took me in when I was near death—after running away from my Indian captors. They were kind to me. Accepted me. Let me marry one of their maidens and have my own family. When she and her family and friends were killed, they didn't blame me. Unlike you, Mr. Thompson."

Captain Jones stormed off leaving the crowd behind him speechless.

"I didn't. I meant... Oh heck, why did he twist my words."

"He didn't twist anything, Pa. Can't you see he's been to hell and back," Becky spat out.

"Watch your language, girl."

"Paddy, enough. We owe Captain Jones our lives. If it wasn't for him, how many of us would be sitting here now?"

"Exactly, Pa. You should be thanking the man not judging him and finding him wanting. I am ashamed of you."

She ran despite her ma shouting at her to come back. She had to find him.

"I CAN'T BELIEVE you could say those things, Pa, after everything Captain Jones has done for us."

"Leave your pa alone, Johanna," Rick's tone was harsher than he usually used.

Johanna opened her mouth but a look from Rick made her close it again. He stepped toward her and took her hand.

"We have a decision to make. Clearly this man Mitchell and his friends are a danger to this train. To all we hold dear. We must be prepared for an attack at any moment."

"If Captain Jones was no longer our leader, Mitchell wouldn't have any reason to target us."

David turned on Mr. Newland, the expression on his face as savage as his tone.

"How can you even contemplate such a thing? Captain Jones has done nothing to deserve such disloyalty. After all that man has been through, you would cast him off? Leave him to fend for himself?"

"Of course he wouldn't. My husband was just thinking aloud. He has an unfortunate habit of doing so." Mrs. Newland stepped in front of her husband as if to shield him. "There will be no more talk of anyone leaving this train. We have made it this far together. We are going to Oregon as one group or not at all."

Johanna could have laughed at the formidable expression on the older woman's face, if it were not a moment of crisis.

"Well said, Mrs. Newland. I, too, shall not go any further unless Captain Jones remains in charge," Rick said giving Johanna's hand a tight squeeze. "We all know the dangers that we could face before we get to our destination. Mitchell and his friends will not make me forsake a man I respect and admire."

"Me neither."

"Nor me. There isn't a kinder man alive than Captain Jones. He could have made us stay at the fort after my husband was killed but he didn't. Instead, he kept us a part of this train even hunting for us so we didn't go hungry. I will not repay that loyalty by turning my back on him now," Mrs. Long said before adding, "Jessie, his friend has been more than just a driver. He has been so kind." Tears streamed down the woman's face.

Jessie turned red. "I have worked for the captain for nearly two years. He has always been fair with me— more than fair. I helped him capture that rat Mitchell the first time around. I would have killed that man, most of us would have. But Jones, he insisted on bringing him back to face justice. Look where it got him."

Johanna fought back tears as one by one everyone in their group pledged the same, including her pa, although he was the last to do so.

"David, perhaps you could go find Becky and Captain Jones," Rick suggested before turning to the other men. I suggest we all make sure our guns are clean and ready for use."

"I know how to shoot, Mr. Hughes, my pa showed me."

"But you are a—" Johanna started to say before Rick interrupted her.

"Thank you, Almanzo. Your skills may come in useful, although I do wish you had remained with the children like I asked. I was looking on you to guard them."

Almanzo gave a little sigh before running back in the

direction of the Hughes' wagon where Sarah and the older Long girls were entertaining the younger children.

"I hate to say it but we may need him. We aren't many and none of us are seasoned killers," Rick said grimly.

"But you are not alone."

Ma and Mrs. Newland shrieked as an Indian came out of the wooded area. Johanna ran toward him to give him a hug, forgetting the eye watering scent. She hugged him tightly. "I am so glad to see you. Have you been trailing us?"

He nodded, looking over her shoulder at the group behind her.

"Everyone, this is Paco. He is brother to Captain Jones. He will help to protect us."

CHAPTER 33

*B*ecky followed Scott as he stormed off. She couldn't blame him for being annoyed with everyone, especially her pa. She was glad she was wearing pants as he walked fast when angry. She called out to him a couple of times. Whether he heard her or not, she wasn't sure as he kept walking. Finally, he stopped and she caught up to him, so winded she had to wait to catch her breath.

"You shouldn't have followed me, Becky. I need to be alone."

"Aren't you sick of being alone?" she demanded.

"What do you mean?"

"You are always shutting everyone out. You need friends, Scott. People who care about you. Love you."

"I don't have time for any of that. I need to find Mitchell."

"For what?"

"He has to die for what he did, Becky. Can't you see that?"

"Not really. I mean I believe he should be punished, but I don't see that as your job. You did your best to bring him to justice. What happens to him next is between him and his God."

He stared at her in disbelief before turning away. "Go back to camp, Becky. You're a girl, you'd never understand."

She pulled him around to face her, anger flowing over. "Don't you dare talk to me like that. We feel pain just as much as you do. So I haven't lost my family, and I know I am very lucky. But if I did, I would want to kill the person who murdered them."

"Then you know why I have to find Mitchell."

"No I don't. You are throwing away a whole future on a man who doesn't deserve it. How will killing him make you feel? Better? Is it going to bring back your wife or children?"

When he stayed silent, she screamed at him.

"No, it isn't." She started thumping his chest with her fists. "It will destroy you. Us. Our future. Why can't you see that?"

He stood still as she took out her frustration on him. Finally, she stilled. She looked up into his face. His eyes were full of pain and betrayal.

"Scott, I love you. I love you more than I have ever loved anyone. I would go anywhere with you. So long as we are together."

She reached up on her tippy toes and brushed her lips across his.

SCOTT'S SELF-CONTROL broke as her lips touched his. He put his arms around her, drawing her closer to him. Kissing her wildly, he let his lips roam down her throat, sucking and licking as he went. His body tightened with need as she pushed her soft curves closer to him. He loved her so much. They could have a wonderful life together. He closed his eyes and for a second he could see happiness. It was so close he could almost touch it. But it wasn't for him. It wasn't his destiny.

Scott pushed her gently away from him despite it taking every ounce of self-control not to bed her first. She didn't deserve to be used like that.

"Becky."

"Umm," She responded, her eyes half closed, her body trembling with desire.

"Becky, we can't. We have to go back. I love you, too, but we don't have a future. Not together. I'm sorry."

Becky's eyes widened as his words sunk in. She

pulled away from him, her arms wound around her body. "What? But... I don't understand."

"I'm sorry. I can't." He turned back toward the camp. "We best get back the others will be looking for us."

He couldn't meet her eyes but knew she was staring at him. He could feel her eyes burning into his skin. He didn't want to see the hurt lurking in their depths. It would match the pain in his soul.

CHAPTER 34

When Scott returned to the camp, he found everyone staring at a group of Indians. Johanna and David had moved forward to greet Paco but everyone else looked wary.

"My brothers have been trailing you for quite a while. We have seen no sign of the black hearted devil or his friends," Paco said in his faltering English.

"The what?" David asked.

"My family call Mitchell the Black Hearted Devil," Captain Jones said as he took two strides to reach his brother. "I am so glad to see you, but why are you so far from the village?"

"The Chief ordered me to find Mitchell. My best chance of that is to follow you."

Although Paco's words didn't inspire confidence, Scott laughed. The others stared at them. It took him a few seconds to remember they couldn't understand what Paco was saying.

"Paco was sent by our chief to protect us," Scott explained. It wasn't the full truth but what they didn't know wouldn't hurt them.

"Captain Jones, I owe you an apology," Mr. Thompson said. "I should never have spoken like I did. I hope you will forgive me."

"It's forgotten," Scott said tersely.

"We have been talking," Becky's father continued.

Scott clenched his fists knowing this was the moment when they would dispense with his services. Again, he would find himself outside the white man's world.

"Captain Jones, we want you to lead us to Oregon. Every one of us knows how to shoot and will make sure we are ready to fight this Mitchell whenever he turns up."

Too shocked to reply, Scott just looked at the group in front of him before looking to Becky. She was looking at him, her expression so sad, his heart felt like it was breaking in two.

"If Mitchell turns up. There is no guarantee he isn't on his way back East where nobody knows him," David said, his words meant in reassurance but his tone not quite matching it.

"I vote we continue as we are. We can be vigilant but

let's just assume Mitchell has crawled back under whatever rock he came out of. I don't think we should let a horrible man like that take away our focus from what's important. Getting to Oregon," Mrs. Newland said. Her tone and stance warning nobody to argue with her.

Scott rubbed his eyes which were watering due to the dust. Nothing to do with emotions or at least that is what he would continue to tell himself. He had never experienced loyalty from white people like what he had just witnessed. It was humbling.

"Go, my brother. We will watch your back," Paco said softly. "Be safe and when you finally find your head and decide to marry, I will be at your wedding."

He returned Paco's embrace and then watched his brother leave. He felt Becky move closer but he couldn't look at her. He'd hurt her deeply. She couldn't or wouldn't understand he had to destroy Mitchell.

"What did he say?" she questioned.

"He will watch our back. Mitchell won't take us by surprise."

"Took him a long time to say that. Did he say anything else?"

"No." He couldn't look at her for fear she would see his lie. Paco and everyone else may think he should give up on Mitchell but he was determined to find him and get justice for his family.

CHAPTER 35

The next few days passed by without any further upset. At first everyone was looking behind them as if expecting Mitchell and his friends to be following. As time went on, they became more concerned with the difficult terrain. Becky woke up on yet another cold morning. She desperately wanted to stay under the cover, the air outside was too chilly. It seemed as soon as they had spotted Mt. Hood and Mt. St. Helens in view behind it, the weather turned wintery. She put a sweater over her shirt and pants. She put on her moccasins last before going outside, thankful for their comfort and warmth. She wondered how their Indian friends were coping with the weather but then they would be used to it.

The ground was covered in white frost and when she went to get some water, she found it had formed an ice covering. She blew on her hands to warm them up. It was only early September but she guessed this was a warning of just how cold it could get in these mountains. She quickly built up a small fire and set breakfast on to cook. They had agreed to take turns starting breakfast. Pa had suggested they should try to reserve as much of their strength as possible. It was a good suggestion but she wished she hadn't got the coldest morning. Still, it was pointless thinking about that now. Soon the others would be up and they would be off on another day of travel.

"I need coffee. I can't remember being so cold. Where did all that frost come from?" Johanna said as she came out of the tent yawning.

"It will warm up later. For now, we just need to eat and get moving. Scott said he wanted us on the road early. He wants to make as much progress as possible."

* * *

THE CAMP MOVED OUT and traveled along rolling but good roads with few obstacles. Spirits were high despite the threat of Mitchell and his friends. There was a feeling of anticipation as Oregon—their final destination—was growing nearer.

"I want to get to the Grand Round Valley before nightfall. We will camp there. The mountain ascent will begin tomorrow," Scott said to David as they were riding ahead of the train.

"Is it as difficult as they say?" David asked.

"Depends a lot on the weather. But let's just say I would prefer to put the Blue Mountains behind us as soon as we can."

"Scott, have you decided what you will do in Oregon?"

He didn't want to answer David.

"Scott, I asked you a question."

"I heard you. You know the answer. It's pointless repeating it."

"When you kill Mitchell, what will you do? Even if you get away with murder, you won't be able to settle in Oregon. There will be a price on your head."

"I know that." Did David think he was stupid? He might not have grown up in the white man's world but he knew their rules.

"I don't think you do. You can't have thought this through. I've seen the way you look at Becky and she at you. You are throwing away a wonderful future for a man you claim to hate." David spoke quickly as he tended to do when angry.

"It's none of your business." Scott didn't want David voicing his own fears. He stayed awake at night as his dreams were dominated by Becky.

"Like heck it isn't. You are my friend and if you are

too dumb-headed to know what you are doing is wrong, then I have to tell you." David lowered his voice, "listen, I kind of understand what you are feeling. As far as I am concerned my pa killed my ma."

Scott threw David an incredulous look.

"Don't look at me like that. I am telling the truth. He didn't kill her with a knife but it may have been kinder. She was about to give birth and knew there was something wrong. We didn't have much money but he could have got a doctor. Instead, he went drinking and stayed drinking. He left me and my brother alone. Ma and the baby died." David took a couple of seconds to continue. "It was horrible. He came back drunk. He didn't even care. As soon as we buried Ma, my brother took off. I haven't seen him since. I lost count of the amount of times I could have killed my old man but I didn't. I refused to let him ruin another life."

Although David's story was tragic, it wasn't the same. Mitchell had killed white emigrants on a wagon train just like the one his white family had been murdered on. Then as a direct result of his actions, he'd lost his Indian family. Two families, two chances of happiness gone because of one man. "It's not the same. What if someone killed Eva?"

"I would want to kill them…maybe I would in the heat of the moment. But I wouldn't plan their death, not years later." David paused before saying quietly, "at least that's what I hope I would do. It's something I would rather not think about."

David turned back toward the wagon train leaving Scott alone with his thoughts.

SCOTT RODE BACK INTO CAMP, his belly rumbling with hunger. They would be in Oregon in three weeks at the most. He hoped and prayed the worst of their trials were behind them. He wanted everyone in the group to complete the journey safely.

He caught sight of Becky walking toward her parents. The pants she wore did nothing to hide her curves. In fact, they had the opposite effect. He dismounted, his thoughts making his position uncomfortable. He should head to the stream to cool off. First, he wanted to make sure his horse was properly looked after. Almanzo usually fed him and brushed him down. Since being at the Indian camp, it was almost impossible to separate the boy from the horses.

CHAPTER 36

*H*e wandered around the camp checking on everyone as was his habit. Nobody was ill and most were well-prepared for the trek ahead. He heard raised voices coming from Becky's family so he walked toward the noise.

"Sit down, Rebecca Thompson, and listen to me."

"No, Pa, I don't want to hear it. You're wrong," Becky said, her clear voice carrying in the wind.

"I am your father and you will listen."

Scott winced at his tone. He wondered what Becky had done now to upset her pa. He didn't want to interrupt but that meant staying in the shadows. He didn't feel right eavesdropping on a private conversation. He was about to leave.

"Scott is a decent man. Surely you can see past everything else."

"I didn't say he wasn't decent. I said he wasn't a suitable match for a well brought up young lady. You can aim much higher than an orphan raised by Indians."

"It wasn't his fault. How can you blame him for what happened years ago?" Becky's tone should have warned her Pa, she was in a right temper. "And as for being brought up by Indians, they taught him well. How many times has he used those skills to help us?"

"Your pa is right, Becky. Captain Jones isn't the right man for you. For one thing, he is too old."

"Old. He is only twenty-seven. Ten years older than me. I love him, Ma. I can't live without him."

"Now you are being dramatic. You barely know him. There are plenty of suitable young men living in Oregon."

"How do you know that? You haven't been to Oregon. Anyway, I don't want a suitable young man. I want Scott," Becky insisted.

Scott's heart rose in his chest. She really did love him. Despite his background, his status as an orphan, his unusual upbringing. None of it mattered to her. She was fighting for the both of them. What was he doing? Was he putting her first? He didn't want to answer that question. He wanted to leave but he had to hear what her parents said despite himself.

"Stop that this instant. You will do as you are told. Now go to bed."

"I am not a child, Pa. I won't give up on Scott. I don't care what you think."

Scott's heart was beating so loudly he thought they might hear him. It hurt to think a man like Thompson would hold his past against him. But then he had said similar things when the group was discussing whether to keep him in charge or not over Mitchell.

He walked away slowly, fighting the urge to grab Becky and race away into the sunset. Just the two of them. To go somewhere nobody knew either of them. They could be happy together. If they were given a chance.

He loved her already but hearing her profess her love for him tore his heart apart. But he couldn't fight for them. Not with Mitchell still a free man. It wasn't just because of what the man had done to his Indian family. Becky would never be safe with him alive. Mitchell knew him. He would know to attack Becky would be the way to inflict the most pain possible. No, he had to leave her be for her own sake. But he couldn't ever explain that to her. She was so feisty and stubborn, she would insist on being together regardless of the risk Mitchell posed.

CHAPTER 37

Scott didn't see Becky after her argument with her parents. He didn't purposefully avoid her but the terrain became more difficult.

Everyone had their faces covered with a cloth of some sort. The dust was very fine and troublesome. The ground was difficult for the oxen as there were many deep holes which were almost impossible to fully avoid. Those who could walk did so to help reduce the burden on the oxen. Everyone was exhausted but nobody whined. They didn't have the energy.

"Do you think we will see water soon, Jo?"

"I guess we will, Sarah. There is grass ahead and where grass grows, there has to be water."

"I hope it doesn't smell as bad as it did last night. The stench reminded me of the outhouse at our old school."

Johanna smiled at the younger girl's reminiscences.

The smell from the sulphur springs had been horrendous and caused more than one person to be off their food. But at the moment, they couldn't afford to be too choosy. Water was scarce. She knew her pa was getting anxious about his cattle as were the other men in the group. The women were worried about the children. Her ma had given up trying to keep clothes clean.

* * *

FORT BOISE HAD BEEN SUCH a disappointment. The only things for sale seemed to be sugar and tobacco, neither of which would help nourish them or build up their strength for the weeks ahead. Rick had said Captain Jones hoped to be able to trade with some Indians for fresh fish. It would make a welcome change to their diet of bacon and beans. They were all fed up eating the salty meat but particularly now when water was so hard to come by.

Johanna glanced over at Becky who was riding for a change. She was still dressed in Joey Freeman's clothes having won the battle with their ma. The pants were much more suited to traveling. Johanna wondered what Rick would say if she started wearing them. She was worried about Becky and it had nothing to do with the water or food situation. Her sister's eyes had lost their joy in life. She was very quiet too. Johanna smiled as she remembered how often she had wished Becky to stop talking and settle down, but now she had, she didn't like it. Something had happened between her and Captain Jones. He grew moodier by the day. She wanted to ask but something about her twin prevented her initiating such a private conversation. Instead, she decided to speak to Eva. Maybe David knew something. He had become quite friendly with Jones.

"Are you all right, Jo? You keep frowning."

"Sorry, Sarah. I'm fine. Just thinking that's all." She smiled down at the ten-year-old who had now fully recovered from her illness. She smiled much more than she had done. She no longer trailed after Rick either. Now she was convinced he wasn't going to abandon her and her sister, Carrie, she was happy to let him out of her sight. She kept quite close to Johanna, though, but that was on Rick's instructions. The trail through the hills had many hidden hazards and he didn't want the girls venturing far alone.

Rick and the girls ate at Ma's campfire every night. Johanna was glad her fiancé and father were getting on so well but she missed the companionship they had shared when she had been helping Sarah cook. Now they seldom got a moment alone. She looked up at the mountain in front of them. They had to cross that and then they would be in Oregon territory. They were almost at the end of their trail.

CHAPTER 38

"The track is very winding isn't it Becky? I don't know how you can handle the wagon."

"Plenty of practice, Ma," she said feigning confidence she didn't feel. She knew her ma was worried about their provisions and the weather. She wasn't about to add to her concerns.

They traveled slowly through the winding rocky ravine. Becky didn't look to her left or right but kept her focus on the oxen in front of her. She couldn't think of anything but getting out of these mountains.

David was in charge of the train today as Scott had gone ahead. Becky couldn't help but be glad he was gone, seeing him every day just punctured her heart a little more. But at the same time, she was worried about him scouting on his own. What if he met Mitchell?

There would be nobody to help him. To her surprise the camping area David had chosen was covered in good grass. There was also fresh water. They couldn't ask for more. Ma cooked breakfast. She was better at stretching the rations than anyone else.

Becky helped her pa with the animals. Stephen had run off and couldn't be found but they weren't worried. Her little brother always disappeared when there were chores to be done. He would come back when the food was dished up. His stomach wouldn't let him miss a meal.

"Becky, why don't you take a nap in the back of the wagon. David wants to check some of the wagons and your ma is cooking. You look done in, girl."

"Thanks Pa."

Becky climbed wearily into the back of the wagon and lay down but it was no use. She couldn't sleep because her dreams were consumed by Scott. In the good ones, Becky dreamed Mitchell just showed up one day, all alone. He and Scott fought it out. Scott won and they were finally free. She didn't want to think of the nightmares where Mitchell killed Scott. Losing him, even in her dreams, was too painful to contemplate.

She had barely shut her eyes when she was called for breakfast. David told them they expected to reach the banks of the Colombia river by the afternoon. They would wait there for Captain Jones to come back.

* * *

DAVID CLARKE GATHERED the group together to discuss the best route forward. Captain Jones had explained the options and pros and cons of each before he went ahead to get more information.

"The best way through is over the mountain. Barlow has gone but his toll road is still open. The alternative is to go down the Columbia River but I don't like that option. For one, there is a backlog of wagons waiting to travel. It will take at least ten days to clear it." David looked at his father-in-law. "Secondly, I think you have too many cattle to risk it. The mountain route should be safer."

"How much does it cost?"

"Used to be five dollars per wagon and ten cents for each head of horned cattle, mule or ox. Captain Jones has gone ahead to see if he can negotiate a lower cost."

"Hope so, or I might just have to slaughter all my cattle here. I can't afford those rates."

"Pa! You wouldn't do that, would you?"

"Course he wouldn't, Johanna, he's just complaining about money. Your pa was born worrying." Della stroked the arm of her husband letting everyone know she was trying to ease his worries rather than add to them. The fact they were arriving in the winter months was causing concern for everyone. They had to make sure they had sufficient money and provisions to last until they could start reaping their crops next summer.

* * *

Captain Jones returned having agreed to a special deal with the operators of the toll gate.

"It will still make a dent in your resources but it is the best I could do."

"Appreciate your efforts, Captain Jones."

Becky saw the look of surprise closely followed by pleasure on Scott's face. He wasn't as immune to people's opinions of him as he let on. It bothered him her pa seemed to hold his past against him.

She wanted to go to him, to tell him it didn't matter but she couldn't. He had made it quite clear he didn't see a future with her.

She turned back to the task in hand. Her ma had used the chance to catch up on some chores, and it was Becky's job to restock the wagon after the meal. Their provisions were quite low, but they were hopeful with good management they would last until they got to Oregon. She could scarcely believe the long trip was nearly over. It had only been five months but in ways it seemed so much longer.

"Becky, can you drive the wagon?" Pa asked her. "I

have to round-up the cattle and your ma is with Milly. Seems she has started having pains."

"Poor Milly. She was hoping the baby wouldn't come till we arrived in Oregon." Her pa didn't respond having already walked away. Like most men, he stayed as far away from the business of birthing babies as he could.

Becky climbed up into the wagon seat and gently drove out. Mr. Bradley was driving in front with Mr. Newland behind her. They kept a steady pace though the road wasn't great. She wondered what the toll gate owners did with the money they earned as it certainly wasn't spent on road maintenance. Scott rode up beside her.

"You all right? You look tired."

"Thanks for the compliment. So do you. I guess we all do."

He didn't rise to her bait. He was so infuriating at times. But he did look exhausted. He couldn't still be worried about Mitchell. If he had come after them, he would have done it ages ago. It was pointless taking extra risks attacking a wagon train so close to a big city.

"Well?" she asked.

"What?" he said.

"Did you just ride up to tell me I looked tired?"

He had the grace to blush slightly. "I was just checking up on you. Like I do with all the drivers."

"Sure, I bet you told Jessie he looked tired."

"Nah, Jessie has done this trip as many times as I have.We've worked together a long time. I know he is okay," he said.

She knew he was deliberately avoiding talking about them.

She bit her tongue despite wanting to scream. After everything they had shared. She could play that game too.

"Well, you best get on to check the others."

She was pleased to see the surprise in his face. She waited for him to argue with her but he didn't. He just looked at her sadly before riding off.

CHAPTER 39

They traveled for hours not stopping to take a break. Becky guessed Scott was looking for good camping ground but wished he would hurry up. Her hands and shoulders were sore. She wondered how Milly was faring. Poor girl was probably terrified.

Finally, she heard the bugle calling them to halt. The wagons didn't circle, there wasn't enough space. They parked where they could.

"Thank you, Becky. You did a great job," Ma praised her.

"How's Milly?"

Her ma tried to hide her concern but failed miserably.

"What?"

"I don't like the fact her pains are so strong, yet she

doesn't seem to be in labor. I told her to rest and let us do her chores. You don't mind helping out?"

"Of course not, Ma. But how could she be in pain if she isn't having her baby?"

Becky knew about babies being born, she was the daughter of a farmer after all. But she had never been present when a baby was born.

"Sometimes a woman has pains weeks before the baby comes. Its nature's way of making her ready."

"You don't think that is the case this time?"

"I don't know, Becky. I sure wish Ma Cleaver was here."

Becky screwed up her nose. She hadn't liked the Virgil midwife. She was a cranky old woman who ordered everyone about. But she knew a lot about birthing.

"What about Mrs. Newland? Can she help?"

"Why didn't I think of that. Good girl."

Becky wiped the spot on her forehead, her ma had just kissed. Surprised at the open display of affection—rare in her ma—she went about her chores smiling.

THE NEXT MORNING, they traveled toward the Deshutes of Falls river, a stream about one hundred and fifty yards in width. It was fast flowing so they took advantage of the ferry service provided by some Indians. This time, Captain Jones didn't know them nor did he make any attempt to speak to them.

"Why isn't he trying to speak to them, David?"

"He says he is not sure whether they favor white people."

'But they are ferrying people across the river."

"They can take our dollars without having to like us Becky."

Becky supposed that was true. Once they crossed the river, they had to travel up a long, fairly rocky hill.

"I don't like it Becky, it's too steep."

"Milly, you will be fine. Stop worrying," Becky said all the time thinking you might as well tell a river to stop flowing. Milly would be worrying until her baby came. Maybe it wouldn't stop then.

AT FIVE MILE creek they spotted Mt. Jefferson for the first time. "Seeing Mt Jefferson is making me feel so close." Ma wiped her eyes with her skirt. "After everything we have been through we are nearly there. Our new home is just waiting for us."

Becky didn't respond. Her ma knew the mountainous terrain separating them from their new home included the infamous Laurel Hill. Everyone on the train including the children knew of this hill, named after the trees that grew on it. Or tried to grow would be more accurate as it was so steep only the most hardy trees survived. All the guide books mentioned Laurel Hill and none for good reasons. It really couldn't be as bad as they said it was. Could it?

They traveled all day without water but nobody complained. There was little point. They knew they would get fresh water as soon as the scouts found a good source and not before.

Captain Jones came riding up to speak to Pa. "We need to get down this steep rocky hill and we will be at Village Creek. You can buy potatoes there."

"Della did you hear that? You will be able to cook me some spuds tomorrow."

"I live for your pleasure, Paddy. The highlight of my day is cooking potato mash for you."

The group laughed at the antics between her parents but Becky couldn't smile. More than anything she wanted Scott to love her as much as her pa loved her ma. She couldn't imagine her pa letting something like revenge come between him and his missus.

"How much?" Becky asked.

"Nine dollars a bushel."

Becky gasped. "What are they made of? Gold?"

Scott chuckled at her attitude but stopped as she looked at him crossly.

"Don't shoot the messenger. I didn't set the prices."

"I hope you told him we wouldn't pay. That's robbery," Becky wrinkled her nose in disgust.

"Sure I did, and he was so upset he said he would give them to you."

As Becky raised her eyebrow he threw his hands up.

"What do you expect? Wagon trains are always hungry and low on provisions by the time they get to this spot. He knows he has a market. If you don't buy them, someone else behind you will."

"Let them. I refuse to pay those prices." Becky could have bitten off her left hand for some of her ma's mashed potato but she wasn't giving in to someone taking advantage of them.

"Since when did I die and leave you in charge, my girl?"

"But, Pa, those prices…"

"Are the going rate. Show me where this farmer is, please, Captain Jones. I could do with some of my Della's potato mash. Just the thing to put us back on track."

Scott gave Becky an I told you so look. She stuck her

tongue out at him having made sure first her pa wasn't looking. Scott burst out laughing as he rode off.

* * *

PA GOT his potato mash but Becky didn't eat any.

"Sticking to your principles making you hungry yet, girl?"

"No, Pa," she said just as her stomach decided to grumble loudly. Everyone in the group laughed, even Johanna. She threw a dirty look at Scott who was laughing loudly before storming off to her tent. Men. She was sick of the lot of them.

The next morning, they had to face another trial.

"The slope is dangerous as it is so steep. You need to take things really slow, Mr. Thompson. Slower than slow."

"What sort of idiot do you think I am? I can drive a wagon."

"I know that, sir," Scott said soothingly. " I'm not trying to be disrespectful. Just trying to warn you is all."

"Sorry, son, I didn't mean to bit your head off. I'll take it easy."

Becky bit her lip, not because she didn't trust her pa. She did but the slope was so steep it felt as if she could fall over if she looked down too far. She took Milly's hand on one side, Johanna was on the other.

"We will be fine if we take things very slowly," she said reassuringly as they started to walk down. Traveling in the wagon was too dangerous.

Milly was so white she would have blended in with the mountain tops. "Leave me here. It's too dangerous. I will make you fall."

"We go together. How many times do we have to tell you? We are all part of this group. All or nobody." Becky insisted.

"You can do this, Milly, we believe in you, don't we, Becky?"

Becky was too busy watching Scott to reply. His role was the most dangerous of all. She prayed hard he would be safe. He looked up catching her watching him. He winked but before she could react he had disappeared.

* * *

SOMEHOW, they all descended safely without accident. Becky stood at the bottom of the slope wondering just how they'd done it. It looked even worse looking up at it than it had looking down.

"Was that Laurel Hill? It wasn't too bad was it Captain Jones?"

"No Mrs. Clarke, that wasn't Laurel Hill. Believe me you will know it when you see it." He paused. "We are about seven miles away from Barlow's gate at the foot of the Cascade mountains. I would like to reach that this evening before we make camp."

Everyone made a greater effort to achieve the goal he set. Becky admired them for their tenacity. She knew they were tired, hungry and fed up of bumping along in the wagons. But it was nearly over. Unfortunately the worst part was yet to come.

"We did well today, didn't we?" she asked Scott as he passed by.

"Yes, Becky, we did. Everyone did a great job."

"Scott, can we go for a walk later?"

"I don't think that's wise, do you?"

"I want to speak to you. I think you owe me an explanation." Her heart pounded as she spoke. She was being very forward. If her ma knew what she was doing, she would be in trouble for the rest of her life.

"I guess I do. Later, at the river. Just don't fall in. It's cold."

"I might just push you in," she returned quickly.

He walked off laughing, leaving her seething. Why did he always laugh at her even when she handed out insults? He was the most maddening man she had ever met.

THE RIVER WASN'T LARGE, a small stream, really, just ten or so yards wide. It wasn't even that deep not that she intended to go in to check. She sat at the edge thinking of everything she wanted to say but couldn't. She had to let him talk. He knew how she felt. She'd shown him often enough. Her face burned thinking of their previous encounters. If he kissed her tonight, she wouldn't be able to speak at all.

SCOTT WATCHED from his hiding place. She was so beautiful even when mad or when her face was screwed up in concentration as it was now. He saw her looking at the river and guessed she was wondering just how deep it was. He hoped she wouldn't try to check. It was cold, colder than most rivers even at this time of the year.

She wanted an explanation which was only fair given how he had treated her. His mind flew to the kisses they had exchanged. His body grew hot. If he continued thinking that way, he'd need to take a dip in the river. But what was he going to tell her? Not the truth that was for sure. He didn't relish telling any woman he was choosing to hunt down a murderer over her, but telling Becky was even worse.

He walked to where she sat, moving slowly. He knew she had seen him but she wasn't smiling. This was going to be harder than he thought.

"Becky, I…I am not sure what you want me to say. I told you already we can't have a future together. You have to forget about me."

"I can't. I've tried, God knows I have but I can't. I love you with every fiber in my body. I know I shouldn't tell you but I don't play games. I think you love me too. I know you do."

He stared into her eyes. He opened his mouth to deny his feelings but he couldn't lie to her.

"Becky, I love you…"

Her face blossomed as the worry fell from her eyes, making them sparkle with happiness. Now he felt like a flea on a piece of … "Becky, I can't. I have to find Mitchell. I have to finish what he started."

"I'll wait. However long it takes. I will. I can stay with ma and pa. Help them. Then when you get back, we…"

"Becky, I might not come back. I want you to find someone else. Forget about us."

"No. You can't do this. Make a decision now. Him or me."

She was so beautiful standing there, her defiant pose at odds with the stricken look in her eyes. He wanted to tell her he chose her but he couldn't.

"I thought you were braver than this. I thought

together we could conquer the world but I was wrong. You may love me but not like I love you. I wouldn't let anyone come between us. Yet you've chosen him, haven't you?"

He didn't answer. He didn't have to.

CHAPTER 40

*J*ohanna and Rick walked to the top of the valley. They were desperate to spend some time alone but it wasn't possible. At least the children were playing some distance from them.

"It's beautiful up here, isn't it?" Johanna asked looking at the mountains covered with heavy timber. She spotted pine, cedar and cottonwood trees.

Rick murmured something making Johanna slap him gently. "We are not even married and you are already ignoring me."

"Never. I was just thinking."

"I was wondering how I could carry some of this white oak to Oregon with us. It would make a beautiful bed."

Her face flushed at the look in his eyes. He leaned closer and gently brushed his lips against hers. She looked around her for the children but they were scattered around them, too interested in their surroundings than to be bothered by a kiss.

"Was that what you were really thinking about?"

"No. But it is more interesting than what was on my mind."

Johanna swatted him gently. "What were you really thinking about?"

He took her hands, looking into her face.

"How long it will take to set up the first school? Where it will be? We should try to find some land close to your parents and your sisters."

"You mean file a claim?"

"Yes, why not? It would be nice to have our own place away from the school, wouldn't it? I can see the girls and Almanzo riding horses."

"Horses, our own place? Do you have bags of gold hidden away you haven't told me about?" Johanna asked him, her tone playful.

Rick shrugged his shoulders.

"Rick?"

"I have a little money. My grandpa left me some in his will. Well, he left it to Pa but when he died it passed to me. I was going to give it to Sadie to help her get started if we didn't find Toby. But now it's ours. I was going to use it to set up all those schools I spoke about but..."

"You've changed your mind?"

"Yes, and it's all your fault. I can't bear to be away from you for weeks at a time. The two days you spent at the Indian camp were the longest of my life." He sighed dramatically making her smile. He kissed her gently again. "I know the children of Oregon will need schools but that will have to be someone else's destiny. I want to be with you and our children all the time. To see you every day."

She squealed before wrapping her arms around him.

"I take it you agree?" he asked kissing her on the forehead.

"Yes, oh yes. I agree. I want my own home with a pretty garden and a large barn. Horses for the children sound wonderful. Maybe we can get some from Captain Jones. He might even give us a family discount."

"You still think him and Becky are a match?"

"Have you ever seen two people fight so hard to stay away from each other? I think they will get married just as soon as someone knocks their heads together."

"Spoken like a true romantic."

She pulled him down toward her and kissed him, gently at first before increasing the pressure. His blood roared as she dropped butterfly kisses around his face and down his neck before returning to his mouth and kissing him. He tightened his grip on her as she moved closer to him.

"Yuck, they are kissing again." Carrie's voice echoed causing them to spring apart.

"You know that house we were discussing. Can you make sure the children's rooms are on the opposite side of the kitchen to ours!"

She giggled, her laughter bouncing off the mountain walls too. He took her hand, and smiling, they returned to where the children had been picking berries. He scooped Carrie up in his arms as they made their way back down to camp.

"The view from the mountains is amazing, isn't it, Jo?"

"Yes, Almanzo it is." She was pleased to see the light in his eyes. He had recovered physically but the sadness in his eyes was taking longer to shift. They hadn't seen any sign of his parents along the trail. She was torn between wanting to know what had happened to them and hoping for his sake they would never know. She didn't think his ten-year-old mind could cope with much more heartache. But then, wouldn't it be better to know if they were dead than to live a life expecting them to turn up at some point? She hoped she wasn't around if Mr. Price did walk back into camp one day. She was sure she would be tempted to slap him. Hard!

Almanzo was very gentle and kind with Carrie but seemed in awe of Sarah. He stayed as far away from her as he could but his eyes followed her everywhere. Rick thought he might have a crush on his niece. Johanna hoped that was all it was as he reminded her a little of a young David Clarke who had fallen for Eva a long time ago. If Almanzo came to live in the same house it could make life a little difficult.

She gave herself a mental shake. There was no point in borrowing trouble as her granny would say. They had yet to reach their new home.

CHAPTER 41

They couldn't pull out the next morning as a storm blew up. There was no way Scott was taking the wagons across a dangerous path in the middle of a storm. He told them it was a rest day. He knew they didn't believe him but they played along. The women got caught up on laundry while the men hunted and were surprisingly successful.

"Are you certain we are facing a storm? I don't mean to question you but rations are so low, we need to get to Oregon as soon as possible."

"I know that Mrs. Thompson and believe me I would not be taking this precaution unless I deemed it necessary." At the worried look on her face, he continued in a kinder tone. "You are a good woman and a wonderful wife and mother. We will make it through. You just have to trust me."

"Oh I do Captain Jones. If it wasn't for you, I think we would all be buried on the trail. I didn't mean to upset you."

"You didn't Mrs. Thompson, those clouds did that."

He pointed at the sky and suggested she get under the canvas cover for shelter. The storm came as he had predicted, the rain coming down in torrents. Scott toured the camp making sure all were present and as much as possible protected from getting wet.

"Getting wet ain't going to kill me," Stephen protested when he told him to get back under shelter.

"No but freezing to death certainly will. I am not taking any risks young man now get."

Stephen looked as if he wanted to argue but reconsidered his position at a glare from Scott. Just then he caught Mrs. Thompson looking at him and smiling. He smiled back before checking on the rest of the wagons.

THE NEXT DAY it was as if the rain had never happened. The sun was high in the blue sky, not a cloud in sight. Mt Hood was gleaming in plain view from the camp. Despite the sun, it was cold. There was a cutting wind coming across the mountains. Everyone wore as many layers as possible to stay warm. Becky was very thankful to Winona for the cured hides she had given them. They kept them warm at night.

"Tomorrow we will reach the foot of Laurel Hill. You will need to be brave and not let the sight of the hill intimidate you."

"You've crossed it before haven't you, Captain Jones?"

"Yes Mrs. Newland, more than once."

"Well if you can do it, so can we."

It was lovely to hear the older woman sounding so confident but a quick glance at Scott's face told Becky, he was worried.

"Descending this hill is the worst part of the journey. We need to inch down as carefully as possible. The wagons will slide down the hill, the wheels locked to curb their speed. Rick, David and myself will secure them each with a 40ft tree behind them to slow them down."

"I assume we won't be traveling in the wagon will we?"

"No you won't Milly. You will walk down with the other women and children. You will have to be careful, but you know that already."

Becky knew he was trying to reassure Milly but as she had found out, it was pointless. Milly would only feel better once it was all over.

"Does anyone have any questions?" Scott asked.

Nobody responded so he sent them to make camp early. They needed their rest for the trial to come.

* * *

THE NEXT MORNING the camp was full of bleary eyed travelers. It looked like nobody got any sleep. Becky tried to prepare herself for the trial ahead. They had no choice but to travel down the hill.

"Is that it?" Milly shrieked. "Alright for him to say we should be brave but look at that. It's almost perpendicular. There is no way a wagon can travel down it. How does he expect an ox or us to walk down?"

"We could always sit on our bottoms and sled down." Becky's attempt at humor partially worked.

Everyone laughed apart from Milly who looked scared stiff. She didn't blame her friend. Despite her joke the hill was scary. It was about a mile long.

"The stream runs down one side, and as you can see there are large loose rocks here and there, so be careful. I don't want to have to fish anyone out of that stream, it's cold."

"Yes Captain Jones," they chorused. Well, all apart from Milly who'd been struck dumb.

"The men will bring the oxen and horses. The animals will get distressed but I want you ladies to concentrate on nothing but getting yourselves and the children down. You are the most important." He looked at the group. Becky felt his gaze linger on her but she refused to look at him.

"Mrs. Thompson, how on earth are we going to walk down?"

"Milly, you have to trust Captain Jones. He knows what he is doing. Now come with me."

Rick carried Carrie, behind him Johanna walked with Sarah. Becky was with Almanzo, Eva following with Stephen. Becky kept a close eye on her ma and Milly but despite a few close calls, they all made it down safely. The women waited at the base as the animals were next to travel down.

Becky didn't think she would ever forget the frantic struggling of the horses as they made their way down. Their frightened eyes staring at her as if to ask why they had to take this route. She had to close her eyes to their suffering and that of the oxen. She wasn't the only one if the sound of weeping around her was any indication.

It was a long, trying day but they all survived. Every animal, wagon and most importantly of all, her family and friends. They owed it all to one man. The man she loved with every fiber of her body.

CHAPTER 42

*A*lthough the worst of the climbing was over, they didn't make much progress on a daily basis through the mountains. Becky thought of the days when they had covered fifteen or more miles. Now they were lucky to cover six. The weather was against them, it rained almost continuously for days. At night, the rain turned to sleet and sometimes snow.

The real snows would come next month making people nervous. They'd all heard rumors that as much as 50 ft of snow could fall and wanted to be in their homes in Oregon by the time the snowfall started.

There wasn't enough fodder for the animals, and they couldn't get the oxen to eat the leaves from the nearby trees no matter how hard they tried. The trail was strewn with bones of animals , at least they hoped they were. They didn't want to think of the implications.

Captain Jones did his best to keep everyone cheerful.

"This area is called the Devil's Backbone, you can see the ridges look like the bone in your back. We should be able to find some fish in the spring over there."

The boys gathered around Captain Jones begging him to show them how to catch the fish. Becky watched as he patiently showed them again and again how to watch the water.

Almanzo screamed with pleasure when he caught his fish but his screams brought Johanna running.

"What's wrong?"

"Almanzo caught a fish. He's really happy," Becky reassured her.

"Happy? He nearly frightened me to death," Johanna protested trying to get her breath.

"I don't think he thought about that. He was trying to catch one for ages. Scott's been so patient with them all."

"He'd make a good father, wouldn't he?" Johanna said. Becky looked at her twin closely, although her sister's eyes were on the water, she suspected Johanna was trying to play matchmaker.

"You are trying to convince the wrong person, sister dear. It wasn't my choice. He decided he didn't want me." Despite her best effort, Becky's voice quivered with her unshed tears.

"Really? If he doesn't care for you, why is he making such an effort to look good in front of you?"

"I don't know, Jo, but I am fed up trying to work out what he wants. I have decided I am going back to Virgil."

"What?"

"You heard me."

"But you can't. Not after we came this far," Johanna insisted.

"I can and I am. There is no future in Oregon."

"But you will meet someone else. They say there are about ten men for every woman out there."

"I don't want anyone else. He doesn't want me. I am not going to sit around waiting for him to change his mind." Becky sighed loudly. "As soon as I turn eighteen, I am going to find a group heading home."

"You can't. You've seen the go-backers on the trail. They are totally demoralized and unhappy."

"So?"

"Becky, don't make sudden decisions. There is still time for Captain Jones to come to his senses. Whatever his reasons are for not courting you, when he clearly cares for you, you need to give him time to sort them out."

"Always the optimist, aren't you? I'm sorry, Johanna, but I think any chance I had of happiness is gone."

Becky turned away from the look of sympathy in her twin's eyes. She couldn't bear to be sitting here watching him any longer. She headed back toward the camp. Her ma would have some chores for her to do.

Anything to keep her busy and get him out of her thoughts.

* * *

"THERE IS A FARM UP AHEAD. The farmer is willing to sell us some vegetables and butter if you would like to stop."

"Like to stop? Are you crazy? How long has it been since we had fresh vegetables?" Mrs. Newland answered testily.

"I take it that is a yes please do stop Captain Jones," he said teasing.

Mrs. Newland's face lit up like a red beacon before she realized he was teasing. "Oh, you are mean to me, Captain Jones."

"Well, that just takes the biscuit. Here am I offering to provide luxuries such as corn and potatoes and you are accusing me of being nasty."

Mrs. Newland kissed him on the cheek making Becky giggle as Scott looked so uncomfortable.

"You are the best wagon train leader around and don't you forget it. Now come on, show us this farmer."

Scott went off with Mrs. Newland, and the other ladies followed him like ducklings after the mother duck.

"Are you not going to see the farm?" Johanna asked her twin.

"No. I will leave that pleasure to Ma."

"Becky, you know what you said about returning to Virgil? You weren't really serious, were you?"

"Yes, I was, Johanna."

"Is it truly over between you and Captain Jones?"

"I don't think it ever started. Not really," Becky whispered, not able to hold her emotions back. "I don't know how I will ever get over him, Jo. I love him so much."

"Come here to me."

Becky let Johanna take her in her arms and cuddle her like she did to Carrie and Julia. She didn't know how she would bear her life without Scott in it. She waited in camp with Milly while the rest of the ladies hiked out to a farm Captain Jones had pointed out to them earlier.

THE LADIES RETURNED from the farm laden down with vegetables of every description and three fresh chickens plucked and ready for the fire. Becky watched as Scott set the chickens to roast over a large open fire. Her ma and the other ladies peeled and prepared the vegetables. There was a party atmosphere in the air. Even the children got involved, collecting some berries to serve as dessert. Although it was a simple meal, everyone complimented the cooks. She didn't say anything. The chicken stuck in her throat and she didn't touch the

vegetables despite the butter Ma had added to the potatoes. She wasn't hungry but she didn't waste the food.
After forcing down a couple of mouthfuls, she gave the
rest of her plate to Stephen. He seemed to have hollow
legs as he was always hungry.

She went for a walk mindful to stay within sight of
the others but desperate to get some time to herself.
Scott wouldn't come find her. She seemed to have
become invisible in his eyes. It didn't matter what she
did, he never took her to task for driving too fast or too
slow. He didn't complement her or tell her off. It was as
if she was dead to him.

CHAPTER 43

"That's it?"

Eva's disappointment was shared by most of them judging by the looks on their faces. Oregon City was nothing like they expected.

"It's built in a canyon."

"Never mind that. Look how small it is. I thought it would be a lot bigger." Johanna looked at the long narrow town lying in front of them.

"It's getting bigger all the time. But for now, it is best you ladies avoid it."

Captain Jones came over to stand beside them.

"Why?"

"Would you listen to me if I just said because I told you to?"

Becky colored before looking away. Why did she have to say anything?

"Oregon is still relatively new. It will take a while before it catches up to the law and security you enjoyed in Virgil. I am not sure if we even have a sheriff at the moment. There are a lot of single men in town who haven't seen a white woman, or should I say a decent white woman, in a very long time."

"Your message is clear, Captain Jones. I will not risk my wife's or daughters' safety. I suggest we camp some way outside the town."

"Thank you for your support, Mr. Thompson. We can leave a couple of men to guard the camp at all times. We can take it in turns to go into the town. You will all want to file claims or buy provisions, perhaps both."

"Isn't it exciting? Our journey is almost over and we made it. All of us." Eva smiled happily at David who held her hand. "I just wish Granny was here to see it too."

"Glad Mam isn't here. She would have been totally unimpressed," Pa's disappointed tone made everyone smile but they didn't dare laugh. He looked far too cross to take that in good humor.

* * *

"YOU MAY WANT to live with your parents for a while after you turn eighteen," Rick whispered to Johanna.

"Why would I do that? I thought you couldn't wait to get married."

"I can't but your pa is right to be concerned. We have to file our claim, build a house and a barn as well as a thousand other chores before we will start earning. I want you to be comfortable."

"Don't start our life making decisions for me."

"I thought that was what husbands did."

"This is eighteen fifty-two now. I have a mind of my own. I don't care if I have to live in a wagon and a tent so long as we are together. As soon as my birthday comes, I want you in the church in front of a minister."

"Yes, ma'am," he drew her closer before whispering in her ear, "I love it when you get so bossy. It's a side of you the others don't get to see too often. They think Becky is the only willful one in the family."

"I think they have lost that notion. I am not sure any of us are the same people we were when we first set out on this trip."

Rick's glance fell on the children. Julia Long was playing with Carrie, and Sarah. Almanzo couldn't keep his eyes off Sarah. Their lives had certainly changed.

"Don't worry about them. They will be fine too," Johanna said.

"Has Mrs. Long decided what she is going to do?" Rick asked. "David said she was considering a place beside his, but he thought she would be better off in town."

"Don't think David expected the town to be like this one. That doesn't matter now anyway."

"Why?" Rick looked bemused.

"Were you not there when Mr. Bradley asked Mrs. Long to marry him? It was really sweet. He just blurted it out in front of people," Johanna told him.

"The poor man, he must have been nervous. What did Mrs. Long say? Yes, I guess."

"I think Mrs. Long was torn between giving security to her girls and having a new life, and being disrespectful to the memory of her husband," Johanna replied. "It took a while but she said yes."

"I am sure her husband would want her to be happy. Life is for the living."

"I am so glad we got through. When I think of how close I came to losing you, that day on the river..." Johanna shuddered.

"Well, don't think too badly of the river. It got me to see sense and talk to your pa. Nothing like a near-death experience for setting your priorities straight."

Johanna pushed him away from her pretending to be angry. "Are you trying to tell me you had to nearly die before you knew you loved me?"

"No, darling. I knew that from the start." He kissed her, brushing his lips with hers just like a feather. "Coming to Oregon and meeting you was our destiny."

"Do you believe that?"

"What? In destiny?" Rick asked.

"Yes, that your life is predetermined from the day you were born."

"Not really. I believe we all have choices and those decisions we make will shape our destiny. Why are you asking?"

"I was thinking of Becky and Captain Jones. She said she is going back to Virgil as soon as she turns eighteen. She is going to live with Granny. I don't know if she will bear it."

"She will, Jo. Your sister is a tough nut. And I wouldn't give up on Captain Jones just yet. Maybe he needs a near-death experience to see the light too."

"Rick Hughes, that's a dreadful thing to say."

* * *

Becky saw her sister and fiancé laughing and kissing. They were so happy and she was glad for them, but she couldn't help feeling a little envious. Her gaze drifted around the group. So many happy couples making plans for the future. Milly's baby would be born any day and Stan was fussing over his wife, driving her to distraction. Eva and David were still caught in the post honeymoon bliss, their eyes rarely losing sight of each other for long. Even Mrs. Long and Mr. Bradley had a happy ending. Why couldn't it be like that for her and Scott?

Darn that Mitchell guy to... She couldn't finish that thought despite what the man had done. Where was he anyway? He hadn't attacked them as expected on the wagon train. Paco and his men had shadowed them for miles but it was as if Mitchell had disappeared. Maybe he had run off, frightened Scott would come after him.

She looked down at the town—her family's new home. What job could she find there to help her get the money to go back to Virgil? Even if it was safe for her to go into Oregon City, what would she work at. Her sewing skills were enough to get by but she didn't have the skills to open a dressmaking shop. Her cooking skills weren't too good either. She could run a boarding house but she didn't have the money to buy one. Anyway, her pa wouldn't entertain that idea. A single woman didn't entertain overnight, male guests. It was so hard being a woman. If she was a man, she could get a job with horses or other animals. She could become a sheriff. She liked the idea of bringing law and order to a town. But nobody had heard of a female sheriff. Just what was her destiny?

CHAPTER 44

They had set up camp some miles outside town. People were in a festive mood and the women had cooked up a feast. The men had found provisions in Oregon City while the boys had gone hunting so they had everything their hearts desired, everyone apart from her.

Becky was fed up of the party. The people she had traveled with for months had reason to celebrate but what did she have? Feeling sorry for herself, she decided to go for a walk around the camp.

She kept walking, not realizing she had gone further than she thought. She was about to turn back when she heard someone call her name. Looking around, she couldn't see anyone. Thinking her mind was playing tricks on her, she turned to go back toward the wagons when she heard it again.

She looked closer at a clump of trees in front of her. A man lay on the ground, and had been there for some time by the look of him. She rushed over without thinking.

"Miss Thompson. You got to help me. I got to go get my boy."

"Mr. Price. You're alive. Are you hurt? Wait here and I will go get help."

"No, stay. Please. I ain't got long left."

"Don't talk like that. Almanzo will be really happy to see you. I will just go—Ouch!" Becky's hand was twisted behind her back just before a less-than-clean hand covered her mouth. The smell made her stomach roil.

"Gentle now, miss. We don't want anyone to get hurt, do we? Not yet anyway." She pulled away from the sound of his voice in her ear. "Now don't be so unfriendly. Been a long time since I held a woman this close. I aim to enjoy it."

Becky lashed out with her foot and gave him a good kick on the shins. It was worth the ache in her foot to hear him cry out.

"Cut that out you little…"

"Can't handle a woman, Bill. You forgotten how? Want some lessons."

The evil voice made her skin crawl. Mitchell. The man from Fort Hall.

"Yes, it's me. You recognize me, don't ya?" He leaned

in closer to her. "Come for your gentleman friend I have. Me and him got business to clear up."

Becky bit through the hand covering her mouth and screamed for all she was worth before a clout from Mitchell knocked her senseless.

"Gag her and tie her up with the others."

The others? Who else had they already caught?

Becky fought like a wildcat but it was no use. She sensed the man holding her was enjoying her reaction so she stilled. She needed to conserve her energy and use her brain to get her out of this mess. They were after Scott. She had to warn him.

She saw Price jump to his feet, nothing wrong with him that a bath wouldn't clear up. She could have growled with frustration. He had tricked her and she'd fallen for it.

They dragged her for a bit but when she kept tripping up on purpose, her captor lost patience and picked her up like a sack, hauling her over his shoulder. He carried her back into the woods before dumping her in the clearing. Looking around she saw two men bound up tightly. Her eyes widened as she recognized Paco and Beaver. Paco looked at her and then looked away as if she was of no interest to him. Beaver didn't look up at all. They were pretending not to know her. She didn't know why but they had to have a reason. She was going to go along with their pretense.

"You know our friends don't you, Miss Thompson, or shall I call you Becky? I hear that's what you prefer."

Becky threw her questioner a dirty look. She couldn't say anything with the filthy gag in her mouth.

He pulled it out but kept his fingers away from her teeth.

"I asked you a question," Mitchell said.

"I don't answer stupid questions."

She was rewarded with another slap.

"I'll have some fun teaching you some manners." His leering eyes frightened her but she was not about to show him. She pretended indifference hoping he would lose patience and move away. Then she could go looking for her knife.

As if he read her thoughts, he started to pat her down.

"Got to be careful these days, don't you? All sorts of people carrying weapons including innocent looking ladies like yourself."

She nearly cried when he found her knife. Taking it, he stole a kiss.

"That's just a taste of what's in store for you."

"You touch me again and I will kill you," she spat back at him.

"Mitch, leave her alone. We got work to do."

"You're just jealous, Bill. You can't wait to get your

hands on the twin sister. Or was it the elder one you wanted."

"Her twin is mine. He can have the married one. Johanna Thompson owes me some respect and I know just how to teach it to her," Price called out.

Becky rolled and vomited just over Mitchell's shoes. He kicked her in disgust. She rolled away from him, not to protect herself but to save her energy. She was so angry she couldn't see straight, never mind concentrate. How dare these men talk that way about her sisters. She caught Paco's eye. He was trying to give her a message but she didn't understand. Then he called out.

"White men are so brave. Picking on little white woman. No wonder our braves kill them so easily."

She closed her eyes at the beating his words earned him. Surely her family and friends had realized by now she was missing. They would come and find her, wouldn't they? But then Scott would be in danger. There was no mistaking the hatred Mitchell had for him. After all this time, they'd thought he was behind them, but he'd been waiting for them. He was like a fox—cunning. It made him all the more dangerous.

"Enough. I don't want him dead. Yet," Mitchell ordered.

Bill and Price let Paco go. He slumped to the ground as if he had lost consciousness. She prayed he was pretending to be more badly hurt than he was as he looked awful. She looked at Beaver but he was still staring at the ground. Surely, he would do something. Anything.

CHAPTER 45

*S*cott wandered around the camp stopping to talk to people when they called to him. He was grateful they had all arrived safely but he couldn't relax. He didn't know if it was because now his job was done he would leave to seek out Mitchell, or if it was something else. He hadn't heard from Paco in four or five days. It wasn't unusual enough to be a sign of something bad but he couldn't shake the feeling his brother was in trouble. Maybe the army had launched an attack on the village. He wished his brother and family would move higher into the hills. There was a system of caves they could use to provide shelter in the worst of the weather. They would also serve as good hiding places but the Chief refused to run as he saw it. The medicine man had accused him of being a coward for even suggesting it, but he'd sensed the Chief understood his reasons. But the Chief couldn't afford to lose face with his tribe. Not now, when so many of them thought he was weak for not fighting the white man.

Scott went to get some water and found David by his side.

"Oh, you are here."

"Of course, where did you expect me to be?"

David looked sheepish and somewhat embarrassed.

"David?"

"Have you seen Becky anywhere?"

"No, why?" The feeling something was wrong intensified.

"Becky's been missing for a while. When we couldn't find you, we assumed, that is to say we thought…"

"You thought we were together. I haven't seen her alone tonight. I don't like this David. You know what she is like."

'You don't think she would have gone into Oregon City, do you?"

"Not likely but then she is so impulsive you never know. She would have taken a horse. Can you check whether one is missing? I will go find Rick and a few of the other men to come with us if we have to search for her."

David moved quickly to check the horse situation

Captain Jones turned to find Johanna in front of him. She was paler than normal, her eyes troubled.

"Becky is in trouble I can sense it. It's a twin thing. You have to help her."

"Can you tell me where she is?"

"No. But she is scared. Oh please, Captain Jones. Find my sister."

She impatiently brushed away a tear rolling down her face.

"I will do my best. When did you see her last?"

"Becky went for a walk. She seemed upset but didn't want to talk. She wanted to be alone and promised to stay in sight of the wagons."

"Since when did your sister ever keep her promises?" His sharp tone lead to more tears. "Sorry, Miss Thompson. That was unforgivable. Can you please ask Rick to join me? I need some of my men to come with us."

She nodded but before she could move, he added, "I will leave it to you as to what you tell your parents. But wait until we are gone. Your father will be in no condition to go searching in the woods at this time of night."

She turned away and hurried to find her fiancé. He looked quickly around the room, signaling to a few of his regular men.

"Jessie, we got trouble. Miss Thompson, Becky, has disappeared. I smell Mitchell."

Jessie paled. "What do you need boss?"

"More men. Got any friends down in the city?"

"Yes, sir, a few. I might be lucky to catch them before they drink the bar dry."

"Go fetch as many as you can. The sheriff, too, if there is one. I don't know if they replaced Murphy after he got shot in the robbery. Make sure you bring men you trust. I don't fancy getting shot in the back."

"Sure thing, boss. Don't go getting shot up before I get back. You ain't paid us yet."

Jessie's grim humor worked to reduce his tension level slightly. He needed to concentrate. Maybe Becky had just lost track of time. But he sensed it was more than that, although for once he hoped his senses were wrong.

CHAPTER 46

He went to mount up when he heard a whistle he'd recognize anywhere. It was Paco's son, Walking Tall. If the teenager was here, there was trouble. He moved toward the trees, whistling back his own signal. The boy almost fell into his arms, panting hard from exertion.

"They have my father and your woman."

"Where?"

"Some miles that way."

"How many of them are there?"

"Fifteen, although it was dark so there may be more."

"Paco and Becky, are they hurt?"

Walking Tall stared back, his expression saying more than he could put into words.

"I want you to go and tell the men what you have told me."

Walking Tall shook his head. "I am staying with you. Father told me to stay close. He thinks there is more shocks on way."

What could be more shocking than Mitchell having Becky and Paco? He looked to the boy but he returned his stare blankly.

"Have you anyone with you? Where are my brother's men?"

"Father sent them back to our village. There was talk of a raid. I think it was an excuse but I do not know for certain."

He put his arm around the teenager's shoulders sensing his dilemma. Should he do as his father had ordered and stay here or should he go back to his village to check on his father's wife and younger siblings. Walking Tall had lost his mother to a soldier's ambush when he was but two summers.

"Paco knows what he is doing. He said stay with me so that is what you must do."

He paced, wondering what to do next. He couldn't just barge into the woods as he was outnumbered. But the very thought of leaving Becky with Mitchell for one second longer than necessary tore at him too.

"I have idea. Do you want to hear?"

He looked at the boy. Despite his tender years, he was Paco's son, and his brother would have given him the skills necessary to protect himself and his family.

"I am listening."

The boy's plan was simple but potentially lethal to Mitchell, and the chance of success was high despite its simplicity. He introduced Walking Tall to his men and outlined the plan. He didn't mention whose idea it was. Now was not the time to plant any seeds of doubt.

The men nodded as he spoke. "Do we go now or wait for Jessie?"

"We go now. There is no time to lose. We got to smoke these snakes out."

Walking Tall had already scouted the area. There was nobody else living in the woods and there were no wagon trains parked near enough to be affected. Apart from their own.

David came running just as he finished explaining the plan.

"No horses are missing. Oh, hello." David recognized Paco's son. "They have Becky?"

"Yes. Paco too. At least fifteen men with guns. We are going to smoke them out."

"What? You mean to set fire to the wood?"

"Yes, it's the only way. It will give the impression there are more of us and buy us some time until Jessie gets back from town with reinforcements."

David was looking at him as if he had gone mad.

"You can't set the wood on fire. It hasn't rained for days. The whole place will go up in seconds."

Scott smiled.

"What? I am obviously missing something."

"This is why the soldiers always underestimate my Indian brothers. They only see the obvious." At David's puzzled look, he explained. "Mitchell and his men are camping in a part of the woods that just happens to have a natural fire break nearby. All we have to do is extend that break a way around the back of his camp, without being seen, and they will be trapped.

"Have you lost your mind? Becky will be caught in the middle of that fire. Paco too," David protested.

"We will get them out."

"How can you be sure of that? There has to be a better way."

Walking Tall scowled but Scott knew David was worried for Becky. There was a risk, of course. But then Mitchell could shoot Becky as soon as they set foot near his camp.

"It's our only chance of getting her back safe. Do you want to come or stay with the others?"

"I'm coming. Eva and her ma know. They will tell her pa when we go and then they will distribute guns to everyone who can use one. Will they be safe from this fire of yours?"

"Yes." So long as the wind didn't change direction, but he saw no reason to mention that now. They needed to focus on what was happening, rather than worrying about what might happen later.

* * *

RICK CAME UP TO HIM. "Johanna told me. What do you need me to do?"

"I want you to stay here." Before Rick could voice his protest, Scott outlined his plan. "If the wind changes you will have to clear the camp as fast as you can. Can you do that?"

"Yes, but surely you need more help?"

"No, stay here. I can't explain it but there may be other trouble coming. Paco sent me a message but I don't fully understand it as yet. I need someone I trust here. Someone calm who can act under pressure."

Rick nodded. "Come back soon. Safe with Becky and Paco."

The fact Rick included Paco meant a lot to him. He grasped Rick's hand firmly before leading his men into the forest.

He saw Paco's son had done his job well. The clearing was a natural fire breaker and the stream behind it would guarantee it would work. They should be able to fool the white men into thinking the fire was bigger and that a whole tribe of Indians was chasing them. Mitchell knew the Indians hated him, so his imagination wouldn't take too much persuading.

He went to each of his men explaining the plan and their part in it. All the while, his mind tried to work out what Paco's warning meant. What other surprises had his friend discovered? They waited as long as they could but there was still no sign of Jessie. He sent one of his men, Duke, back to camp to wait for Jessie and to explain their plan. Last thing he wanted was Jessie and his friends getting caught in a firestorm.

CHAPTER 47

Becky sniffed, she was sure she could smell something. A fire. She looked around but couldn't see anything. She caught Paco's gaze but couldn't tell what he was thinking. One eye was swollen from the beating and almost closed, the other had a cut right above it. She wished she could help him but her hands remained tightly bound despite her efforts to release them.

"Boss, you smell that?" Price whined.

"Quiet. I'm thinking."

"His brain is working so hard, there's smoke coming out of it."

"Shut up, Bill."

Becky listened to them arguing. The smell of smoke was worse now. It was irritating her nose and the back of her throat. She couldn't cough properly because of the gag.

"The woods are on fire." A man came running toward Mitchell.

"I told you not to leave your post."

"Boss, the woods are on fire. We got to pull out. It's spreading fast."

"Do you think it's the Indians? Jones wouldn't be stupid enough to set the trees on fire when we got his girl here."

"I don't know who it is. Don't care neither," Bill cursed. "We got to get out of here. Look how fast that's moving."

Becky's eyes widened as the flames grew higher. The smoke was denser now. Was this it? She looked to Paco but he was lying still. Was he dead?

Beaver had moved. Not by much, but he was now slightly nearer to Paco than before. Becky caught his eye but he looked away. She sensed he was telling her not to stare at them. She moved her feet focusing Mitchell's attention on her.

"Don't worry, girlie. You're coming with us. Won't leave you here to cook." His evil laugh sounded louder than before. She bit down hard on the gag in her mouth to stop the tears welling in her eyes from spilling over.

He came nearer and roughly pulled her to her feet but as they were still bound she fell over. Cursing he grabbed his knife and slashed through the bonds. "You try anything funny and you're dead. Got it?"

She didn't acknowledge his threat. She couldn't say anything anyway given his dirty rag was in her mouth.

He pulled her closer to him, motioning his men to move toward the area of the forest not in flames.

"I ain't going in there, boss. All those trees, we gonna go up in smoke any second."

"Where do you want to go?"

"The river is that way."

Mitchell followed his man toward the river, dragging Becky alongside him.

"What'll we do with the Indians?" Price asked.

"Leave them."

"Shouldn't we shoot them first?" Bill suggested, his finger on the trigger.

"And put them out of their suffering. Over my dead body. They aren't going anywhere. They are bound tighter than a hog on a stick," Mitchell taunted.

The men laughed again. The tears flowed down Becky's face. She pushed her body in a desperate bid to reach Paco but Mitchell cut her off.

"I thought you was Scott's gal. Developed a fancy for red skin, did ya? Would change my mind if I were you. Dying breed they are." He laughed at his own joke. She kicked him, causing him to trip over. She tried to run but one of his men cut her off.

"You try that again I will shoot you," Mitchell growled, catching up with her. He slapped her across the face to show he was serious.

Becky sobbed as he pulled her away from Paco and Beaver. She gave one last look behind her, seeing the two men lying on the forest floor. Soon the flames would reach them. Where on earth was Scott? Surely, he and the others had seen the smoke? Maybe they were dead. Had the Indians killed them before attacking Mitchell?

CHAPTER 48

*B*ack at the camp, Rick paced around wishing he was out there with the other men. All the remaining men, women, and some of the older children who could shoot were armed. The other children were in place to help load guns if they were able. Mrs. Freeman was minding the very young children in the back of one of the wagons.

"You see anything, Hughes?"

"No, sir. Not yet." Hughes answered Mr. Thompson who was also pacing. He'd put up a real fight, wanting to get into the forest to look for his daughter. It had taken a long time for his wife to calm him down and persuade him his place was protecting the rest of his family.

Johanna came over to stand beside him. He wished he could remove the concern from her face, but until Becky was back safe and well, that wouldn't happen.

"Can you talk to Becky?" he asked not looking at her, aware of how silly his question sounded.

"You mean in my mind?"

"Yes. I know it sounds silly but back East there were a few people who said twins could do that."

"We can't. I can sense when she is in trouble as I feel apprehensive and sick even if I am perfectly safe. I have no idea where she is. I can't close my eyes and pretend to be looking out of hers. We are not witches you know."

"I don't know about that. You got me under a spell."

He hugged her close, feeling the tension in her shoulders. He could see the same fear in Eva, although, of course, she was worried for her husband and sister.

"Rick, I am so glad you are here with me. I couldn't bear it if you were in danger too."

"I feel so useless standing here. I should be helping."

He held her as she rested her head on his shoulder. Then she pushed him away.

"Look, that's smoke. Oh my goodness, the forest is on fire. Oh, Rick, they are going to be burnt to death. What will we do?"

"Nothing we can do but pray. Captain Jones knows what he is doing."

"Someone's coming. Look." Johanna pointed at a figure making his way out of the forest.

"It's an Indian. I think it's the man who helped us cross the river. Maybe Paco sent him," Rick said.

Before he could stop her, she was running up to the Indian.

"Beaver, is that you?"

The Indian gasped for breath. "Need help. Paco hurt."

Rick told Johanna to go back to her pa. He would go with Beaver.

"Get your bag. If he is hurt, he will need nursing."

He didn't wait for her reply but followed Beaver back toward the forest. He could feel the heat of the fire and hoped Beaver wasn't going to direct him into the middle of it.

Paco was lying on his side at the edge of the trees. Rick saw he was badly hurt. He helped Beaver carry him back to the camp where Johanna and Eva came forward to nurse him.

"What's up with him?"

"Looks like he was badly beaten. I sure wish someone could speak to Beaver. He could tell us about Becky."

"She with Mitchell."

Both Rick and Johanna looked at Beaver in shock.

"You speak English."

"Some, not much. I have to go now. Go help."

"But what…" Rick didn't continue as the man disappeared into the forest.

Johanna tended to Paco. Her ma helped as they washed him, fixing him up as best they could. "His leg is broken. I never set a leg before," Johanna said, her voice trembling.

"Neither did I but your pa has on animals. He should be able to do it," Ma answered as she went to get her husband.

A couple of the men came forward. Johanna was thankful Paco was unconscious as the pain of their actions would be horrendous. He remained out of it while her pa and Mr. Newland set his leg. They splinted it. She had it bandaged by the time Paco recovered consciousness.

"Thank goodness, I thought you would never wake up."

Paco tried to pull himself up.

"You are not going anywhere. Lie still."

"I must go find He Who Runs. Danger. Beaver."

"Yes, we know. Scott has gone after Mitchell, Beaver has gone to help him."

"Beaver no help."

"He did, he helped bring you here. You need to rest, Paco. Your body took a beating. I don't know how bad your internal injuries could be."

Paco started rambling in his own language. Johanna tried to calm him but nothing was working.

"What's he rambling about?" Rick asked.

"I have no idea. He says there is trouble. Mitchell and Beaver."

"The poor man. He is horribly injured yet still concerned about the others. Do you have anything to knock him out?"

Johanna's stomach turned. "I can't, Rick. I don't know how to use that type of medicine and I could make him worse."

"Maybe he will wear himself out."

Rick's prophecy came true fairly quickly as Paco lost consciousness again. Johanna checked him regularly. His heart was still beating strongly. The men moved him carefully to a feather bed. That was all they could do for now.

CHAPTER 49

*B*ecky did everything she could to slow Mitchell down. She stumbled a couple of times and tripped him up on one occasion. Each time earned her a slap but it was worth it. She heard other sounds in the forest. Some were caused by animals fleeing the fire. But she'd heard human voices too. Mitchell thought it was Indians but she knew it was Scott. He was coming for her. Maybe he was coming for Mitchell her inner voice taunted but she did her best to ignore it. Regardless of why he was coming he would be here soon.

"Boss, the river is just up ahead. Want me to scout ahead and check it out?"

"Chicken liver. You're just trying to save your neck, Price."

"Want to come here and say that, Bill?"

"Will you two cut it out. The people chasing us won't care who they kill first. We will all go to the river."

"But, boss, what if they are waiting for us. What if this was a trap?"

Mitchell stopped to look behind him.

"We can't go back. The fire has overtaken our camp. We got no choice but to go on. Price, you go check it out. Take Turner with you."

The two men moved forward at a quicker pace. Within seconds, both screamed out simultaneously. A couple of the men ran toward Price.

Mitchell came to a standstill.

"Indians. Up ahead." One of the men came running back, a broken arrow in his hand.

"Did you see how many?"

"No, sir, but sounds like a hundred. Price and Turner are dead."

"It's Jones. He's bluffing. Come here girly." He pulled Becky close to him again, this time removing her gag.

"Go on scream to your man. Get him to come here."

Becky stayed silent.

"I told you to do something."

She stared back at him. She wasn't going to put Scott in danger. No matter what.

"You better scream, girl, or I will make you." He

pulled a knife out of his pocket, the blade glinting despite the limited light.

"You do what you want. I won't betray Scott. Ever," Becky said, her nails piercing the palms of her hands.

"Come on, boss, let's get out of here. Leave her."

"Don't tell me what to do."

Becky saw Bill pale. Everyone, even his own men, were terrified of Mitchell. Well, she wasn't, or at least she was going to make him think she wasn't. She knew there weren't that many men with the camp, so Scott couldn't have too many people with him. Mitchell had at least thirteen guns left. She had to separate the two groups.

"You going to let him tell you what to do? Some leader you are," she taunted Mitchell. "I thought you were supposed to be brave."

"Shut up, girl."

"Make me," she baited him before turning to Bill pretending to flirt with him. "Should I be looking at you as leader? Are you really in charge here? You look more intelligent."

"Enough, shut up."

"She got a point, Mitchell. Since when are you the boss?" Bill spat. "I thought we were equal partners. I say we got to get out of here."

"We go when I say we go."

"You're going to get us all killed." Bill looked at the men around them who were staring back at him. "Are you going to stay here and burn or get murdered by the redskins? Or do you want to follow me out of here?"

"You ain't leaving me like a rat from a sinking ship," Mitchell growled a warning.

"I guess I am."

A shot rang out as Bill fell back, a look of shock on his face. Becky had been waiting for something to happen so she took off running. She ran in the direction Price had taken. "Scott it's me, don't shoot. Please don't shoot."

She almost made it but Mitchell made a flying leap at her feet knocking them both to the ground.

"You ain't going anywhere without me, missy. You're my protection."

"Let her go, Mitchell, you are surrounded."

Becky yelped as Mitchell increased his grip on her while looking around him. Becky couldn't see anyone either but she'd heard his voice. He'd come.

"I ain't coming out there, Jones."

"You scared?"

"Why don't you face me man to man? Just you and me," Mitchell yelled.

"Yeah right. As soon as you see me you will put a bullet in me. What happened to your other men?"

"They are behind me."

"Funny, I thought at least half of them were dead. We got a couple of live ones here, don't we?"

Becky heard a scuffling sound before two men shouted out to Mitchell. One said, "I got jumped, boss. He's got Indians with him. Lots of them."

Mitchell cursed.

"You best let me talk to him. I will get him to promise to let you go," Becky said, desperation making her voice shake.

"Got a high opinion of yourself, don't you? I heard he wouldn't marry you, he was set on coming after me."

"Who told you that?" She protested, wondering how on earth he knew that. Nobody knew what Scott had told her. Nobody other than David and Paco. Paco? He wouldn't have betrayed Scott to Mitchell. He had been badly beaten up but still he wouldn't have turned against his brother. But he wasn't his brother, was he? He was an Indian and Scott was white.

She shook the horrible thoughts out of her head. What was wrong with her? Paco only ever did anything to help her and here she was doubting his loyalty.

"Come out, Mitchell, or my men will go in after you."

"Not much of a choice, is it, Jones?"

"I dunno about that. If you come out, I will shoot you. A fast, clean and quick death. If I send my friends after you, you will be begging someone to shoot you."

Becky saw Mitchell pale as he swallowed hard.

"Wonder if it's true?" she whispered.

"What?"

"Scott told me the Indians can tie a man to a tree and burn him to death without singeing the tree."

"Course that ain't true."

"Horrible thought, isn't it? Maybe they will use ants instead?"

"Ants?" His eyes filled with terror. "Oh, shut up. I can't think with you yapping on."

"I'm losing patience. So are the men. You killed Aged Oak's wife, daughter and son. He really wants to get his hands on you," Scott called again.

As if to reinforce Scotts words, an arrow came flying over their heads. One of Mitchell's men cried out.

"Another one down. How long, Mitchell?"

"You're bluffing, Jones. I have your girl."

"What girl? The Thompson one? Didn't you hear I turned her down. I have a woman. Kateri's sister. Very beautiful and passionate. Unlike any white woman."

Even though she guessed he was trying to protect her, it still hurt to hear him state the truth. He had turned her down. She'd thrown herself at him. She blinked back her tears. She wasn't going to cry in front of Mitchell, even if her heart was breaking. She fell to the ground, her legs giving way as her body shook with stress and fear. But wait, Kateri didn't have a sister.

She'd only had one brother. Her sister had been killed by Mitchell in the same attack that had killed his family. Was Scott sending her a message or was her broken heart making her read things that weren't there?

CHAPTER 50

*J*essie returned from Oregon City with about ten men.

"Where's the boss?"

Rick pointed toward the burning forest. 'He went in there. Some time back. He hasn't returned."

Johanna watched Jessie's face. She didn't know him that well but Mrs. Long had a high opinion of him. She had told her, she thought he might be a good match for Sheila Freeman. Jessie was afraid of the fire. That was a good thing as far as Johanna was concerned. It meant he had a brain unlike some of his friends who just wanted to rush into the fight in the forest.

"He left one of his men to wait for you. I think his name was Duke."

"Thanks, Hughes. I'll just go check with Duke. Some of the men are nervous," Jessie added in a whisper.

"There's been talk of some Indians on the move. They think they may be headed here."

"We have Paco here. He's Jones' friend. Wounded by Mitchell but I haven't seen any others apart from Beaver. But he ran back into the forest ages ago to help Jones."

Before Jessie could check anything, an arrow flew over his head quickly followed by another one.

"Indian attack, get under cover."

Rick dragged Johanna behind the circled wagons. Thankful he had prepared their best chance of fending off an attack, although he had expected white men under Mitchell's control not Indians. Why were the Indians attacking now?

"Rick, look that's Beaver. He's coming in."

"Hold your fire. That man is a friend."

"He's Indian," a man Jessie had brought with him spat out.

"Some Indians are friends. Hold your fire," Rick insisted.

Rick went out to meet Beaver. Johanna bit her lip watching her fiancé with Paco's friend. Paco made a sound interrupting her. He was trying to sit up again.

"Paco, you got to rest. You could die." She pushed him back to make him lie down.

"Don't trust Ahmik."

"Who?" Johanna wasn't sure what name Paco was trying to say. It was obviously an Indian. Was he raving?

"Ahmik."

"Okay we won't. Now will you please sleep. When Captain Jones comes back, he will be very cross with me if you die."

"Son of Medicine Man. Be careful."

Johanna checked his fever. His head was only slightly hot but not enough to cause him to ramble like this. But she didn't show her concerns to him. She asked Mrs. Newland to sponge him down while she went to check on Rick.

Rick was talking to Beaver who was making agitated hand gestures.

'What's all that about, Miss Thompson?"

'No idea, Jessie. I don't think Beaver speaks much English and Rick certainly doesn't speak Indian."

"He's coming back."

Johanna waited until Rick was back inside their camp before running into his arms.

"I was worried about you."

"Beaver wants our guns."

"Why? Are you sure?" At the look on her fiancé's face, she continued quickly. "What I mean is, he doesn't speak English. Could you have misunderstood him?"

"No, he said Jones wanted the guns."

"Captain Jones? He wouldn't leave our camp unattended."

"I know, Johanna, but that's not all."

Jessie cleared his throat. "I know Jones is friendly with the Indians and all, but why would he want more guns and why send someone back who can't speak English? That doesn't make any sense."

Rick and Johanna exchanged glances.

"But Captain Jones introduced us to Beaver. He helped us cross the river. We wouldn't be here if it wasn't for him," Johanna replied.

Jessie shrugged. "I am not saying anything about him but I just don't like it. It doesn't sound like Captain Jones to me and I been riding with the boss for a while now."

"Can we buy some time? I could tell him we have guns hidden in the wagons but it will take a while to find them all." Rick looked at Jessie who nodded grimly.

Johanna looked at Beaver. There was something about him that was bugging her and she didn't know what.

"How is Paco?" Rick asked quietly.

"Oh my goodness, Paco. He said not to trust Ahmik. Do you think he knew Indians were coming?"

"Johanna, wasn't that the name Jones used for Beaver? When he introduced us, we couldn't say his name so he used an English name for him."

Johanna's heart raced faster. "He's trying to hurt us?

But he brought Paco here for help. He would have left him behind in the forest if he meant to kill us. Wouldn't he?"

"I have no idea but we have to stall him. We got to get to Scott and warn him."

"You can't go. Beaver knows you are here," Jessie said quickly. "He will get suspicious if you ride out."

"What do we do then? We need you and your men to help protect us. We have no idea how many Indians are with Beaver. And why are they here in the first place?"

"Their chief said Becky and I would always be welcome in their camp. He said he would always be our friend."

"Never can trust an Indian," Jessie's friend spat out.

Johanna glared at him. Rick told him to shut his mouth.

"I'll go," Jessie said. "You best get back to Beaver and tell him the story about finding the guns. Meanwhile, I will take the men back toward the city first. There is a farm a little ways back. They can wait there. It will look as if we are going on to the bar in Oregon City."

Johanna bit her lip as Rick rode out toward Beaver. She couldn't bear to watch so she went to check on Paco. She bathed his forehead making him wake up.

"Paco, is Beaver, Ahmik?"

Paco nodded.

"Is he trying to hurt us?"

"Yes, hates He Who Runs."

"Why?"

"His mother, sister, wife and baby were killed by Mitchell."

"But Captain Jones hates Mitchell. It is so mixed up."

"Yes. Very big danger. I help." He tried to raise himself up but fell back down.

CHAPTER 51

"Paco, where are your men? Are they attacking us too?"

Paco became very agitated. "No, they go back to camp. Heard story soldiers coming. Need horse. I go get men."

"Let me get them," Almanzo said coming out of the shadows.

"Almanzo, no. You are too young."

"I am not. I am a good rider and fast. I can get help."

Johanna shook her head at the same time Paco nodded.

"Let boy go. Boy take this. It will keep you safe."

Paco tried to take his necklace off but couldn't. Johanna helped him and handed it to Almanzo reluctantly. "I don't like this. You should stay here where you are safe."

"Ain't none of us going to be alive if Indians attack us now,"Almanzo said firmly. "The Indians know me from the last time. They don't know any of the other men."

Johanna couldn't argue with him, it was true.

"Take my horse Al. He knows way home. He is near farm back there. You will know him. Let him smell." Paco pointed to the necklace.

Johanna pulled Almanzo close. "You better come back safe, do you hear me?"

"Yes, ma'am."

"Speak to chief. No one else," Paco gasped trying to speak clearly. "Mother was called Wildflower."

Almanzo glanced at Johanna as Paco lost consciousness again.

"You are very brave," Johanna tried but failed to stop the tears falling.

"I best get going before anyone notices." He gave her a quick hug before he set off running. Johanna watched Almanzo until he disappeared from sight. When would she see him again?

* * *

NOW SHE HAD to find Rick and tell him Almanzo had gone to the Indian camp. Alone. She was not looking forward to his reaction. Rick was talking to Jessie when Johanna came back.

"You don't need to ride for Paco's men, Jessie," Johanna said looking her fiancé in the eyes. "Almanzo has already gone."

"What? You didn't stop him?"

"No, not really. I didn't want him to go but what other chance have we? Jessie needs to find Captain Jones and tell him what's going on. None of this makes sense."

Seeing she was close to the breaking point, Rick took her in his arms. "I won't let anything happen to you, I promise."

Johanna wanted to stay there in his arms, but they had to pretend to be looking for guns. Otherwise, Beaver and his friends would get suspicious.

"Why don't we give them some guns?" Johanna asked.

"What? So they can turn them back on us?" Jessie asked, his expression showed he was wondering if she had hit her head.

"If we give them a couple of old ones, broken old ones, it may buy some time."

"You aren't just a pretty face, are you, Miss Thompson? You mean sabotage the guns."

"There must be a way of doing it so when they try to fire, it hits them or hurts them in some way."

Jessie grinned. "There sure is. Let's have a go at them. Wouldn't mind seeing their reaction when the guns go off."

"Let's hope we don't get to that stage," Rick said dryly, keeping Johanna's hand tightly in his.

CHAPTER 52

How much longer were they going to sit here? It was getting dark and cold. She shivered violently. What was he waiting for? Becky wished for the thousandth time she could speak with Scott.

"Mitchell, I'm running out of patience and my men are getting mighty hungry. You got five minutes to come out here or we are coming in."

She yelled as Mitchell pulled her to her feet. The pins and needles were bad enough but he was holding onto her hair so tightly it brought a tear to her eye.

"Mitchell. What's it to be?"

"You're going to kill me but not before I get to finish her off." Mitchell drew her own knife from his pocket. "She kindly provided the weapon too."

There was no response. Was he going to just let

Mitchell kill her? He wouldn't do that, would he? Mitchell pulled her closer, she felt the blade slice into her skin.

"Any last words?" He leered into her face.

"Yes, you can die in—" She didn't get to finish her sentence as Mitchell tumbled toward her. Shrieking she tried to get out of his way but failed. She fell to the ground under his weight. Kicking and screaming she tried to get him off her but she couldn't.

"Becky, take it easy. We got you. Stop kicking. Jeez woman will you do as you are told. For once."

Scott. It was Scott. He was here. She opened her eyes to see him pull Mitchell from her. He took her hand, pulling her to her feet and into his arms. His hand came away covered in blood.

"He cut you. Where?"

"It's a scratch. Nothing to worry about. You came. You saved me."

"You saved me, you mean. My life is nothing without you."

His mouth fixed on hers savagely.

Someone coughed. And coughed again. They finally came up for air to see David standing there with his hands on his hips.

"As her brother-in-law, I don't know if I should challenge you or congratulate you."

"Definitely the latter. But first we best get her back to her family. They are bound to be worried sick."

"Sure thing, boss. What do you want us to do with him?"

"Is he dead?"

"Yes." At the look Scott threw him, David exclaimed, "He is. I checked. I think you must have hit him in the heart."

Only then did Becky look down to see a knife in Mitchell's back. She turned and retched into the bushes to one side.

"Sorry, darling, I shouldn't have let you see that."

Becky burst into tears. She sobbed and sobbed unable to form a sentence properly. It was over but it wasn't. It would never be.

"Becky, it's okay, darling. We will take you to your ma. You are safe."

"Not crying for me. Paco. He's… He was…"

"Where?"

"Back there. I tried to help him but he wouldn't let me. He said they could roast."

"They?"

"Yes, Beaver was with him. They were both tied up and then the fire came and…"

"Becky, back up. Are you sure it was Beaver?"

"Yes, Beaver was tied up beside Paco. Paco tried to

help me when Mitchell hurt me. They beat him. Really bad. I think they could have killed Paco."

"We have to get back. That's what Walking Tall meant. Paco was trying to warn us. There's trouble on the way."

"What do you call this?"

"Indian trouble, David. Beaver is Medicine Man's son. Medicine Man holds me responsible for the loss of his family when the army attacked."

"You! But you weren't even there."

"I know but you've seen the medicine man. He hates me and he filled his son full of hatred too."

Scott screamed orders at his men. He called for Walking Tall but the Indian had already left. Jessie came running just as they were making their way back.

"Captain, we got trouble. Indians on the attack."

"Beaver with them?"

"You mean the man who helped us cross the river. Yes, sir. He sent a message saying you wanted guns."

"Hughes didn't give him any, did he?"

"Yes, sir."

Scott groaned.

"Broken ones, sir. Miss Thompson, Johanna, suggested we sabotage them first. I got away as soon as I could. I have men waiting at the farm just up the road. The farmer wasn't too happy, so I paid him off."

"Good job, Jessie. I will go to the farm. Can you please stay with Becky?"

Becky's head swung up.

"I am going with you."

"Not now, Becky."

"I am going and you aren't stopping me. That's my family out there. I can fire a gun."

"She's right, Scott. We need her. Do we know how many are attacking?" David asked.

Jessie shook his head.

"How is Paco?"

"Johanna is nursing him but he isn't too good. She's real worried."

"He's a fighter," Becky whispered to Scott.

"Shouldn't someone go find reinforcements, like Paco's men?" David asked.

"Almanzo has already gone," Jessie answered David.

"Alone?" David asked.

"Yes, sir. He headed out to find Paco's horse a while ago. Paco gave him something to show the Chief he was loyal."

"Let's hope the Chief is still alive and Medicine Man hasn't finished him off too," Scott said grimly.

CHAPTER 53

Becky's heart thumped so hard she was sure it was going to burst out of her chest. She'd been scared when Mitchell had her but not as terrified as she was now. Her family was caught in an Indian attack, and because of her the men who should have been protecting them were out here in the forest.

"I'm sorry Scott, this is all my fault. If I hadn't taken a walk, I wouldn't have..."

He pulled her closer against him. "You got nothing to apologize for. What happened was Mitchell's fault. I wish you would stay here, out of the firing line though."

"I can't. I couldn't bear to be away from you, from them. I have to help." She knew she was begging but she didn't care. Too much was at stake.

"All right, but promise me you will hang back. I

know you can handle a gun but there are experienced fighters in the group. Don't get in their way."

She nodded, her gaze centered on the road ahead of them. They couldn't see or hear any sign of the camp yet. But that was good, wasn't it? If the Indians were attacking, they would hear noise.

"I will take my men and go in on this side, you better ride in as if you were coming back from town. That may be enough to stop Beaver and his friends attacking."

"Good idea, Jessie. Thank you."

"Don't thank me. You still owe me wages. Can't let anything happen to you." Jessie grinned before saluting and heading off with his men. Scott explained the plan to David who was relieved as it meant he could be near Eva.

They rode up to the camp calling out to Rick in case he shot them by accident.

"You're back. All of you. Am I glad to see you," Rick spoke so fast it was hard to keep up with him.

"Paco?" Scott asked as he dismounted.

"He's still alive. Johanna's with him. But.." Rick pulled at Scott's sleeve. "Prepare yourself. She's not confident he will recover."

Becky squeezed Scott's hand as his face filled with pain.

"Becky, can you check on Paco for me? I will be there in a minute."

When she didn't move, he pushed her gently. "Go, you will brighten his day."

She went.

"Rick, tell me what has happened. Jessie said you gave Beaver some guns."

"Yeah, broken ones. We had to do something to buy some time. Were we right? Is he going to attack?"

'I am not sure. But yes, probably. I am going to speak to him. Don't let Becky come after me."

Scott mounted quickly. David, who hadn't had a chance to dismount, turned to follow him.

"No, my friend, your place is here. Look after your wife and family. I will be back."

David opened his mouth to protest but Scott stopped him. "If I do not return, please tell Becky I loved her with all of my heart."

And then he was gone leaving Rick and David staring after him.

"What do we do now?" Rick asked David

"We wait." David dismounted. "Hopefully, Almanzo will be back with Paco's men, and Jessie is waiting for a signal. He has ten men with guns. What is the situation here?"

"Everyone who can shoot has a gun. The women are ready to load. Eva too."

"We can't do anything yet. We don't want to jeopardize whatever plan Scott has. Do you want to tell Becky, or shall I?"

Tell me what?"

Becky came forward, her eyes looking around frantically. "Where is he? He's gone, isn't he? Alone?"

"Yes, Becky, he is. He had to go."

"He could have brought me with him."

"It's too dangerous and you know it."

"What am I meant to do now?"

"Wait. That's all any of us can do."

Becky would have sunk to the floor if David hadn't been holding her elbow. He gathered her to him, lifting her up like a child, and carried her to his wife. Eva came running forward.

"Is she hurt?"

"Not seriously. Mitchell cut her on the neck. It needs cleaning. Scott's gone."

Eva paled, making David curse himself for his choice of words.

"I mean gone to see if he can stop the attack," he said quickly.

"Poor Becky. She loves him so. Lay her down here, we will look after her."

They both jumped at a scream from behind her. Ma came running followed closely by Pa. "My baby, what happened to her."

"It's all right, Ma, she's alive. She's collapsed is all from lack of water and rest."

"The blood…"

'Most of it is Mitchell's. Becky has a small cut but she is fine otherwise. Scott got to her in time."

"Where is Captain Jones? I need to thank him."

"He's gone, Mr. Thompson. He said it would be easier if he tackled the Indians on his own." David turned to his wife. "Scott said to keep a very close eye on her. She is not to follow him. It is too dangerous."

CHAPTER 54

Scott made his way carefully toward where he thought the Indians would be getting ready for the attack. He wasn't sure what he was going to do when he found them. If he was still alive, of course. Beaver or his father could easily kill him with an arrow at any second.

What could he say to convince them to go home? To leave the white people in peace. They wouldn't care if he said any killings here would be revenged a hundredfold by soldiers. They believed they were able to fight off anyone. Typical view of young, bloodthirsty warriors of any color or race. Soon they would find real life wasn't like that. But he didn't want that lesson learned tonight.

He ran a slow, calming hand down his horse's neck, at the same time sitting deeper into the saddle. The horse was fidgety having sensed the Indian horses nearby. He pulled back on the reins whispering to the horse, reassuring him all would be well. He hoped he spoke the truth.

"I come in peace."

"White man not know what peace means."

Scott couldn't see who had responded. It could either be Beaver or his father, Medicine Man.

"I do not see myself as a white man. I am your brother. I lived with our people for a long time. My wife and children…"

"You were the cuckoo in the nest. You never belonged. Chief was wrong to let you live. He should have killed you long ago before you brought trouble to us."

"Mitchell brought the trouble. You know that. Your anger and grief are leading you, not your head."

An arrow hit the ground, just in front of his horse. The horse didn't rear, thankfully.

"I came in peace and you hide behind bush. Come out and fight me. Let's end this today. Then the rest of our brothers can go home and beg forgiveness from the Chief."

"The Chief is no longer."

Scott couldn't think about that now. He loved the old man who had been nothing but kind to him. But he had no way of knowing he was dead. For now, he had to concentrate on the task in hand.

"Chief is wise. He not willing to fight white man as he knows it will be the end of our people. He is correct and brave enough to admit what the future holds. If he didn't care about all of you, he would gladly send you into battle."

"You speak as if you truly understand, but you don't. You never did."

Scott dismounted. He left his horse where it was knowing the animal would stay. He walked slowly toward the voice, he now recognized as Beaver.

"You are wrong. I know more than you think. I know you care. You wouldn't have saved Paco if you didn't. You are angry. This I understand. But Mitchell is your enemy not the white people back at the camp. Not me."

Silence greeted his remarks.

"Mitchell is dead. This time for real. I killed him."

Beaver materialized, armed with a knife and a gun. Scott recognized it as Mr. Thompson's.

"You lie."

"No, Ahmik." Scott used the Indian's real name. "I can show you his body. I learned from my mistake last time. Mitchell will never hurt anyone again."

"You killed him because he had your woman. Not for revenge for my family."

"Yes, I did it to save Becky. I also did it for Kateri, Crawling Bear and all our friends and family who died at the hands of the soldiers. I did it for those who died in the wagon trains Mitchell attacked. For my own white parents and brother who died at the hands of Indians." Scott stopped. He looked directly into the other man's eyes. "I did it to stop the killing. On all sides."

As they spoke, more Indians came out of the trees behind Ahmik. They were poorly armed, some carrying the guns from the camp but the majority had bows and arrows. Scott glanced around quickly. He couldn't see the medicine man. There was still a chance to stop this.

"Ahmik, what is it you want?" Scott asked.

"To have our lands back. To be free to live our lives as we have always done."

"How will killing my friends achieve that?"

Ahmik didn't answer. He scowled at Scott. Scott waited a couple of seconds before asking. "Answer me!"

"Just kill him and let's get on with it," an Indian Scott didn't recognize spoke.

"You should know that there are more men with guns waiting for you back at the camp. The rest of our brothers are also on their way back." Scott took a deep breath hoping his next words would get through to Ahmik. "Paco sent for them."

"Paco, he lives?"

Scott didn't miss the hope in Ahmik's eyes. "Yes, Ahmik, thanks to you. He lives. For now." Scott took a step and then another one closing the distance between him and Ahmik. He saw the younger man's eyes full of tears. Gently he took the gun and knife out of his hands. "Come, my brother. We will go see Paco. Together."

Ahmik moved forward.

"No. It is too late. My son has made his choice." The medicine man roared. "I am now ruler of our tribe. There is no place for you."

A shot rang out. Scott flinched but the bullet didn't come near him. He opened his eyes to see the medicine man on the ground. Ahmik dropped to his side, examining him. He raised his face. "He is dead."

Scott moved quickly to check. He put a hand on Ahmik's shoulder. "I am sorry."

Ahmik fell to his knees grieving his father. The Indians around him muttered furiously.

"The Wise One is angry. That is why Medicine Man died. He made bullet come out wrong way. It is a sign," the Indian who had told Ahmik to kill Scott muttered loudly. "We must go back to our camp and beg our chief for our lives. Come. We must go. Quickly."

CHAPTER 55

S cott didn't correct them. Instead, he thanked God for Johanna Thompson.

Hearing horses behind him he whirled around. Jessie and his men, closely followed by the Chief and his men.

"Sorry, boss, but we heard a shot and assumed the worst," Jessie shouted as he dismounted.

Scott nodded to him before going to greet the Chief. "I am sorry. I tried to stop it."

"It is not your fault. It is the way it is supposed to be."

"Mitchell is dead. His body lies over there." Scott pointed in the direction.

"Scott watch out."

At Jessie's shout, Scott whirled around to see Ahmik lift his father's knife. Before he could do anything, the Indian fell on it. He ran toward Ahmik but it was too late.

"Tell Paco. I sorry."

"He knows," Scott said softly holding Ahmik as the breath left his body. He only got up as he heard her shouting his name. Becky. She shouldn't see this. He laid son beside father before turning to the Chief. "I have…"

"Go find your woman. We will talk later." The Chief smiled.

Scott didn't need telling twice. He quickly mounted his horse and rode as fast as he could toward the camp. Becky was running towards him, screaming his name. He jumped off, taking her in his arms and crushing her against him.

"I heard a shot, I thought… Thank God, you are alive."

"I have a lot to live for. Rebecca Thompson, will you marry me?"

She pushed him slightly apart from her, looking up into his face."For real?"

He kissed her, pulling her against his body as their embrace deepened. When the cheering and clapping started, he reluctantly released her mouth but kept her by his side. "Forever."

"Oh, yes." Becky leaned in and kissed him again despite her father watching them.

"Doesn't anyone court anybody anymore? I am not sure I can handle modern living, Della. I need some whiskey."

"Yes, dear." Mrs. Thompson handed her husband a bottle before coming toward the couple.

"Captain Jones, on behalf of my husband and myself, thank you for saving our daughter. We welcome you with open arms to the Thompson family."

"Now I wouldn't go that far, Della."

"Drink your whiskey, Paddy."

With his arm firmly around Becky's waist, Scott moved forward through the crowd of people congratulating them. "I must see Paco."

"Johanna is with him. It will take time but he is going to recover."

Becky took Scott's hand pulling him toward where Paco was waiting.

"Took your time. She will share blanket. Yes?"

"Yes, my brother. She will and you will be there to see it."

"Della, did he just invite the Indian to their wedding night?"

"Paddy Thompson, will you drink your whiskey and whist." Everyone laughed as Mrs. Thompson continued. "He invited him to the wedding."

Scott checked Paco's injuries while filling him in on what happened with Medicine Man and Ahmik.

"I am sorry boy is gone, too, but it is better for tribe. Now we may have peace."

"I hope so, my brother."

Before they could say anything else a baby wailed.

"Milly! I forgot she was having her baby." Becky ran toward a wagon closely followed by Johanna and their ma. The men stayed where they were. Having babies was women's business. Scott took the opportunity to talk to Paco. Paco explained how he had come across Mitchell and how he had suspected Ahmik but couldn't get away to warn anyone. Scott thanked him for helping Becky before telling him the rest of the story.

"Milly has a beautiful baby boy. Both are healthy but Stan could do with some whiskey," Johanna called out to everyone.

Scott and Paco exchanged smiles. Then Almanzo and Walking Tall joined them.

"You became a man today, Almanzo. Thank you for your help."

Scott ruffled Almanzo's hair as he blushed bright red from the praise.

"I almost forgot. The Chief said to tell you he was going home but would expect you to visit in a few days when you bring Paco home. He will speak with you then."

Scott nodded. He had to speak to the Indians, but first, he had business to resolve here. Family business.

CHAPTER 56

*B*ecky returned after mother and baby had been washed and were resting. She had some tea for Paco and water for Scott.

"Go, talk to feisty lady. She has things to tell you."

Scott looked at Becky who nodded. He took her outstretched hand. She asked Johanna and Rick to follow them.

When the four of them were clear of the others and could speak in private, she explained what had happened when she had first been kidnapped by Mitchell.

"I tried to help Mr. Price, I thought he was ill but he was faking. As soon as I went near him, I was grabbed and taken away."

"Price was with Mitchell."

"Yes. He was horrible. Said he wanted to find you and teach you a lesson."

Rick pulled Johanna closer, sliding his arm around her waist.

"He's dead now though. Killed by an arrow."

"Oh poor Almanzo. I wonder where Mrs. Price is?"

"Judging by the way Price looked and acted, I think he was riding with Mitchell for some time. I would guess she is dead too."

"What will we do?" Johanna looked to Rick for answers.

"What we always planned to do. Keep the boy with us. There's no need for him to know what happened to his pa."

"I disagree. I think it's important you never keep secrets. They have a way of coming back and causing problems. Tell him. He is old enough to understand and he believes them dead anyway."

"I agree with Scott. He will only try to find them or expect them to come to Oregon looking for him. This way, its final. It's all over."

Johanna exchanged a look with Rick before she moved to embrace Scott and Becky.

"I hope you two will file a claim near us. Be happy."

She then took Rick's hand. "We best get back to the others and leave those two to work out where their future lies. Last time I heard, Becky was going back to live in Virgil." Johanna and Rick walked away leaving Scott staring at Becky.

"Don't look at me like that. You didn't want me, I didn't know what else to do. I couldn't stay here without you."

"Listen to me, woman, and listen good. There hasn't been a day that has passed since we first met where I didn't want you. Whatever plans you have for returning to Virgil you can forget about right now."

"Really. Who says you are in charge?"

"The law. As your husband, I will tell you where to live. As of now, that happens to be on a horse ranch somewhere in Oregon. No arguments."

"And what if I do want to argue?"

He brought his lips down to hers, kissing her so soundly her whole body tingled.

"You were saying?"

"I have no idea but please do that again."

"This?" he said before claiming her lips again.

In answer, she wrapped her arms around his neck.

When they finally broke apart, she whispered, "I never argue with my destiny."

EPILOGUE

After the events of the last few days, their group decided Oregon City was not the home for them. They moved on toward Portland, where there was less competition for land. The town was also more civilized with more merchant-style stores than saloons and business catering for other needs.

They filed claims next to one another so soon the entire area was owned by members of their wagon train. The men worked together to build a house on each property, having agreed in advance everyone would get a basic homestead. Each family unit could build onto it as required in the following spring/summer when they would have more time. For now, it was important to provide shelter for the winter months.

The locals were friendly, although they had laughed

at Ma's spinning wheel. There were few sheep in Oregon so she wouldn't have the wool to spin.

"We tried spinning the hair from the wolves. We have plenty of those but it didn't work out too well. They aren't as obliging as sheep," one nice woman joked. "Don't look so worried. The local store provides cloth for women's clothing. There's some suitable for men too, although your menfolk may prefer to wear buckskin like the old mountain men."

Becky wasn't sure her pa would be one of those men but she didn't say so. Pa was still smarting over the fact he couldn't afford to pay six dollars for each glass window, especially as Rick had ordered them for the house he was building for Johanna. Ma said she didn't care. They could get a shingle roof and glass windows next year. For now, they had arrived safely and that was all that mattered.

THE FIRST SUNDAY in October found everyone in their group at the local church. If the minister was surprised to find various Indians in his congregation, including a chief wearing his full headdress, he didn't comment. In front of him stood four couples.

"We are gathered here today to witness the marriage

of…" Nobody laughed as he took out a sheet of paper from which he had to read the names.

"Johanna Thompson and Rick Hughes, Rebecca Thompson and Scott Jones, Jessie Chambers and Sheila Freeman, and Mrs. Long and Mr. Bradley."

The couples smiled at each other as the minister gave them the vows which they had to repeat in front of everyone. Nobody made any mistakes which was unusual given the number of people involved. The minister was just about to pronounce them as married when Carrie piped up.

"Are you going to ask them to share blankets? They must be very cold as everyone keeps talking about it."

Even the minister laughed before he pronounced them married in the sight of God. Then he added they should go home and party before they settled down with the shared blankets.

Ma Thompson stood watching her twins walk proudly down the aisle on the arms of their respective husbands. She sniffed a tear back.

"What are you crying for, woman? They're happy, aren't they?"

"Aw leave me be, Paddy Thomson. You never warned me that this was our destiny. To reach Oregon and lose all our girls before we even had a roof on our home."

"We haven't lost the girls, Della. We gained three new

strong strapping sons. Now our roof will be the best and biggest in the whole of Oregon. Just you wait and see."

He offered her his arm and walked her down the aisle as proud as he'd been at their own wedding all those years ago.

THANK you so much for reading the first three books of the Trails of Heart series. I hope you enjoyed the continuing stories of the Thompson girls and the people who come in and out of their lives. Almanzo's story is next:

They thought the Oregon Trail was the hard bit.

The mistakes of the past are impacting the future.

Can Almanzo, now a grown up, take control of his destiny or ...will he let being an orphan destroy his chance of happiness?

He needs to leave what happened on the trail behind him but fate intervenes. Read now Oregon Discovery

HISTORICAL NOTE

The attacks on wagon trains by men masquerading as Indians didn't start until the late 1850s and early 1860s. There were witnesses to two horrific attacks. These happened in different years but at locations quite close to one another. In both cases, some of the emigrants survived. They identified white men who were trying to disguise themselves as Indians. These men seemed to lead the attack which included the Shoshone and Bannock tribe members. People believe these men were so called Land Pirates, intent on stealing valuables and cash from the emigrants.

But those times didn't fit with my story so I borrowed some history instead to explain some of the backstory for Scott Jones. Sometimes my imagination goes wild after reading real life accounts of events. The fact the Indians were blamed and massacred in retaliation had me in tears. Yes, Indians did attack wagon trains but in reality there were far fewer emigrants killed than Indians. And you could say, I suppose, the emigrants were trespassing on Indian lands.

If you would like to read more about the Oregon Trail, there are many books written by the people who traveled. These include these books.

12 Days of Christmas - co -authored series.

The Maid - book 8

Clover Springs Mail Order Brides

Katie (Book 1)

Mary (Book 2)

Sorcha (Book 3)

Emer (Book 4)

Laura (Book 5)

Ellen (Book 6)

Thanksgiving in Clover Springs (book 7)

Christmas in Clover Springs (book8)

Erin (Book 9)

Eleanor (book 10)

Cathy (book 11)

Mrs. Grey

Clover Springs East

New York Bound (book 1)

New York Storm (book 2)

New York Hope (book 3)

ACKNOWLEDGMENTS

This book wouldn't have been possible without the help of so many people. Thanks to Erin Dameron-Hill for my fantastic covers. Erin is a gifted artist who makes my characters come to life.

The ladies from Pioneer Hearts who volunteered to proofread my book. Special thanks go to Nancy Cowan, Marlene Larsen, Cindy Nipper, Marilyn Cortellini, Sherry Masters, Janet Lessley Robin Malek, Meisje Sanders Arcuri and Denise Cervantes who all spotted errors (mine) that had slipped through.

Kirsten Osborne, Cassie Hayes and the incredible group of people who make up Pioneer Hearts, a Facebook group for authors and readers of Historical Western Romance. Come join us for games, prizes, exclusive content, and first looks at the latest releases of your favorite historical western authors. https://www.facebook.com/groups/pioneerhearts/

Last, but by no means least, huge thanks and love to my husband and my three children.

Printed by Amazon Italia Logistica S.r.l.
Torrazza Piemonte (TO), Italy

56166306R00154